Loss Soup
and Other Stories

Nick Hunt

Even though my flowers may yellow,
they shall live
in the innermost house
of the bird of the golden feathers

— Nezahualcóyotl (*Hungry Coyote*)

Loss Soup and Other Stories

Nick Hunt

Cover Design: Christian Brett, Bracketpress, UK
Interior Design: John Negru
Cover art: *Herd (not seen)*. Detail. Daro Montag © 2022

A Greenbank Book
Published by
The Sumeru Press Inc.
PO Box 75, Manotick Main Post Office,
Manotick, ON, Canada K4M 1A2

LIBRARY AND ARCHIVES CANADA CATALOGUING IN PUBLICATION

Title: Loss soup : and other stories / Nick Hunt.
Names: Hunt, Nick, author.
Description: Short stories.
Identifiers: Canadiana 20220134170 | ISBN 9781896559827 (softcover)
Classification: LCC PR6108.U58 L67 2022 | DDC 823/.92—dc23

For more information about Greenbank Books
and The Sumeru Press
visit us at *sumeru-books.com*

Contents

❧

All is Well

❧

The foreigners in our city are taller than we are. When not pacing the streets in the high heat of noon, sweating behind their beards, they cluster together in stiff, upright postures, as if they are trying to see over the walls we have built to keep them out of our plots and gardens. Some people say they stand like this because they are a proud and dignified race of men. Others say it is because they are nervous.

The foreigners in our city wear different clothes from us, and observe different customs. Despite the heat they insist on their heavy hats and coverings, with the result that they always seem exhausted and angry. Yesterday afternoon I saw one, behind the trees on the bank of the canal, remove his cumbersome headgear for a moment to enjoy the cool breeze that blows in from the lake. He looked so fresh, so relieved, that I almost liked him. But when I saw him later, driving down prices in the marketplace, his hat was back on his head and he looked exactly like all the others. Some people say they wear these clothes because they are stubborn and strict with themselves. Others say it is because they are stupid.

The foreigners in our city are all men, and they have thick beards that have grown matted because they don't wash as often as we do. They travelled for many months to get here, and couldn't bring their women to live with them. Perhaps this is why they are always so tense, and stare hungrily at girls from the corners of their eyes when they think we are not watching. Some people say it is dangerous, having young men like these in the midst of our city, without families to watch them, or wives. But there are so many more of us than there are of them.

The foreigners have not always been here. We remember a time before they came. They first arrived from the east in small, ragged groups, gathering outside the city walls, and no one really understood where

LOSS SOUP   Nick Hunt

they came from, or what sort of people they were. And now they stroll our streets in twos and threes, and buy things in the marketplace to take back to their families, and occasionally attempt to learn our language. At night they return to their enclave just beyond the city walls, although the wealthier rent rooms, and a few even sleep in houses they have bought, or have been given. They make no secret of what they want, and we do not blame them for wanting. Some people say that they want too much. But we will always have more than they do.

The foreigners in our city protect themselves well, from us and from each other. Their faces are like statues when they meet us, stern and unsmiling below their long noses, and yet they laugh among themselves like children. They live within our laws, but are scornful of them. They are not meant to carry weapons, but we know that they do, because occasionally trouble occurs. It doesn't happen often. They do not want it. We do not want it; not yet. Some people say we should stop them from coming. Others say we can learn things from them.

The foreigners in our city dislike our religion. This was one of the first things they told us. Some people say they want to change our beliefs, to replace our gods with theirs. But our gods will always be stronger.

Last month we held a large ceremony. Twenty thousand people were involved. Our priests worked from dawn until dusk, up to their elbows, until they were physically too tired to continue. Flutes and drums were heard for days. The temple steps were stained. There were flowers and feasts and chocolate, and the foreigners were invited to witness it all, because we thought it was something they should see. They skulked behind walls and at the edges of the crowd, and refused to eat the food, or to dance. A few became intoxicated and reacted badly. They were generally considered to have behaved very poorly, on such an important occasion. Some people say it was because they did not understand. Other people say they were terrified.

The foreigners have brought foreign dogs with them, although they are not allowed to bring them in the city. Their dogs are bigger than ours, and covered in hair, and they are meant for a different purpose. Some people say that these dogs are being trained; we hear them snarling and roaring down there. The foreigners know we are afraid of them.

Sometimes I try to communicate with the foreigners, but we don't understand each other's languages. I try to ask them what they are doing, and why they have come so far from home, and whether they are happy in our city. They do not seem to know the answers to these questions. I look at their faces beneath all the hair, their sun-damaged skin and pale eyes. Our city is strong, and they are uneasy. We too are uneasy at times.

All is well. Our city is strong. We are waiting, and watching each other.

The Last of Many Breeds

❧

Lily McInnes remembers the day when Donald James Eiger arrived at the zoo – top-hatted, tweed-suited, swinging his cane – and purchased the last of the thylacines for the sum of forty pounds. The beast had been caught in the Florentine Valley three years previously, and had spent its time in captivity pacing and yawning, yawning and pacing, occasionally making a futile leap at the bars and rebounding off them. The zookeepers hated it. It made the other animals nervous, they said – put them off their feed. Visitors steered away from it, preferring the monkeys and the bears, exotic things from foreign lands, not this Tasmanian pestilence. You wouldn't pay to see mongrel dogs exhibited in a cage, so why give money for a sight like that? Yawning and pacing, pacing and yawning, grinning its sheep-murdering grin. The last of its kind, it would never breed – would never produce lucrative offspring to recompense the zoo for the cost of its sustenance and upkeep. All it did in captivity was what it had done in its habitat – consume a small fortune in meat at the tax-payer's expense. If Mr Eiger hadn't made his offer they'd probably have put the thing down, and flung the carcass in the trash with the zoo's other scrapings.

No one knew why he wanted it, but no one knew why Mr Eiger did most of the things he did. A trim, skinny man of advanced years, who dressed like a dandy but never was known to frequent any restaurant, dinner or dance, he was sighted now and then around town, engaged in unknowable business. His money was made in timber, they said – blackwood, blue gum, Huon pine – though some believed he also had dealings with coal, bauxite, gold. He was rumoured to be a mad millionaire, but both his madness and his millions were probably exaggerated. He was certainly rich and strange, and that was enough for Hobart.

Lily, nine years old, watched him arrive in a taxicab and shake begloved hands with the zoo's director. The two men advanced to the thylacine's cage and spent twenty minutes smoking cigars, conversing in low, amenable tones, while the beast stalked back and forward. Then the head keeper – Lily's father – entered the cage with a bucket of meat which he liberally slopped upon the floor, and while the thylacine's jaws were engaged he bagged its head, collared its neck, muzzled its mouth, strapped its legs and fastened it to a length of chain, the end of which he presented to Mr Eiger with a flourish. Three other men half dragged, half carried the struggling thing to the taxicab, where it was pinned against the floor by Simon, Mr Eiger's butler.

'They christened it Benjamin, by the way,' said the zoo's director, again shaking hands. An envelope had been exchanged. 'That's what the papers chose.'

But Mr Eiger shook his head. 'A thing like that needs no name.'

The taxicab left, and Lily watched. It was a blue summer day. She looked back at the empty cage, at her father sweeping up the meat. He turned his head and met her eye. 'No tears now,' he said.

There were different stories told. The house was high upon the hill, overlooking the city and the bay, and not many visitors went to it – but still, the stories travelled. People said it was loose inside the house, that he permitted it to prowl, that it had made a stinking nest in the corner of Simon's bedroom. That it had eaten several cats. That Mr Eiger had *shot* the cats. That constables had visited. That delivery men refused to visit. That Genevieve Eiger, his delicate and perennially ailing English wife, had suffered from nervous fits of some kind and been taken to the hospital. That she might be away for some time. That the servants had departed with her.

There were other stories too. That he was trying to breed the thing. That bitches in heat – dingos, strays – had been brought to the house in recent months and left in a room with the thylacine, but the only thing that remained the next day was bones and scraps of fur. Some said he had taught the brute some tricks – it would yawn on demand when he said 'sleep tight', or fall with its belly in the air when he made a pistol sound. Others believed he had taken its teeth. That he beat it with a bamboo cane, starved it in an airless box, that his ambition was to break its spirit as one breaks a horse's. A gardener from the house next door swore he heard its yowls at night, rasps of fury, screams of pain – and afterwards, the quieter noise of Mr Eiger weeping.

It was strictly not allowed but Lily climbed the hill one day, a half-hour walk from school, into the rich people's neighbourhood, and spied through the iron gate. She could see the big house with its pillars and porch, its gardens dark with Tasmanian oak, but she couldn't see the beast. She wondered if it was dead somehow. If Mr Eiger had punished it too far. Perhaps he had stuffed it, or stretched its tiger-striped skin before his fire.

She stared through the gate for a long while hoping for the truth to come, but no sound, no sign, no shadow came from behind the blank square windows. She walked to the zoo to meet her dad, fibbing that school had kept her late. She passed the thylacine's old cage. An ocelot was there now.

And then there were other, older tales. Tales from before Lily's time. Tales from before Mr Eiger's time, if you counted the years back, but tales that Lily nevertheless believed were connected, somehow. She pictured him as a younger man, uniformed, slouch-hatted, rifle snapped in the crook of his arm, on horseback. On a moonless night. The Black War was long since won but some of the tribes had escaped the Line and continued to live by stealing sheep, haunting lonely stations. Punitive raids on recalcitrant blacks happened in the dead of night, and when they fled their camp fires the raiding squads pursued for days – often using native trackers tamed by money, whisky, church – picking them off with long-range shots from higher ground, from ridges. Like shooting wallabies or cats. This work was rewarded. The ones not shot were rounded up, chained from neck to neck to neck, and marched in dragging, dusty lines to Flinders Island, Oyster Cove, where they were taught to wear clothes and live in proper hous-es. People crowded their doors to watch as the captured blacks paraded past – naked legs, ragged beards, scowling and glistening – an obstacle to settlement, a taint, a dying breed.

Lily had never seen a black. She wanted to, and feared to. Sometimes when she closed her eyes she saw them like a picture show, heads bagged, long limbs chained, in moving lines across the earth. She was too young to remember that. But when she stood at the thylacine's cage, which contained no thylacine, somehow she remembered.

༄

Then the territory was clear, the settlement was won. Frontier families slept without fear of a waddy staving in the door, a spear crashing through the wall. It was a new century. The Irish came, the Cockneys came, the Welsh came, the Germans came. Sealers, whalers, timber-men. Pastures for a million sheep. Rare earth metals, bauxite, gold. The forests splintered to the crash of Huon pine and myrtle.

༄

Sheep were found with their throats ripped out. Ribcages that buzzed with flies. Something else was out there now. The farmers checked their guns again. New rewards were offered.

༄

Three years went by, and Lily grew. Her dad retired from the zoo – he suffered from arthritic pains – and found work on the trams instead. The work was less demanding, and you didn't catch fleas from trams. Hobart's streets were widened, paved. Elegant parks were laid, with rustling eucalyptus. There were streetlights and hotels, more automobiles, fewer horses. Lily's older sister Ruth married, moved to New South Wales. Her brother Sam enlisted in the Royal Tasmania Regiment and was sent to Europe to fight. Another war was starting.

Genevieve Eiger died and the rich people went to her funeral, though most had never been acquainted. Mr Eiger's beard turned white. He was seldom seen in town. People called him a 'recluse' and Lily didn't know what that meant, but it sounded coarse and strange. A bit like 'loon'. A bit like 'loose'. There were rumours of a fight – that Mr Eiger, mindless drunk, had flung Simon's clothes and books from a top-floor window in a thunderstorm, or even attacked him with his cane. Reluctantly, so they said, the butler packed his bags.

Sometimes she thought of the thylacine. It was distant now. She had

14

a picture in her mind, but she didn't know if it was right. A striped backside, a cavernous grin, pointed ears like a dog's – but other than that its distinctions blurred, its features ran together.

No one talked about it now. Perhaps it had only been a silly story told at parties.

Two more years. The food got less. Lily watched the troops parade in Macquarie Street, hung with flags – uniformed, slouch-hatted, with rifles snapped in the crooks of their arms. The men looked strong and brave and clean. The air raid sirens yowled at night. The Japanese were in Hong Kong, Malaya, Burma, Singapore. Perhaps the Dutch East Indies next. After that, Australia. Lily had never seen a Jap. She wanted to, and feared to. Now when she closed her eyes she saw them, at great distances – she picked them off one by one from horseback in her mind.

In the middle of that war, Mr Eiger left the house. Lily wasn't there to see – she learned the legends later.

It was dawn, and he rode a white mare. His silk top hat was at a tilt. He carried a rifle on his back, a waddy in his hand.

They said the beast stalked at his side, or strained ahead on a length of chain. That its flanks flashed in the light – orange black, orange black. That its sheep-destroying teeth gleamed in its yawning skull.

Man, horse and beast passed quickly through the suburbs of the rich and were glimpsed from outlying farms making their way towards the bush. They disappeared, people said, in the woods beyond Mount Wellington. A farmer named Eli Church claimed to have seen them passing by, pausing at a billabong. The horse ate grass, the man drank wine and the beast consumed red chunks of meat, tossed from a leather bag.

The constables knocked at the big house and received no answer. Having forced the door they searched the rooms and reported that nothing was amiss, not a teaspoon out of place. The fireplace was swept and stacked. The marble floors were freshly mopped. Just empty rooms and an open cage – but even that was clean and scrubbed. No clues, just an absence.

Lily McInnes is an old woman now, and she retells the stories. Her grand-children have heard her talk of bunyips, yowies, flightless birds, forgotten tribes of wild men, though these are only fairytales. But sometimes she tells about the man who might be glimpsed on moonless nights, back-country, deep within the bush. They do not like this tale so much but she tells it anyway. Lily changes as she talks. He slaughters sheep, he catches cats. Mad-eyed, he swings a bamboo cane. With tiger stripes across his skin. Upon his head a crown of jaws, hinged open in an endless yawn. No bounty will bring this one in. He is the last of many breeds. The farmers say they'll shoot on sight, until his extirpation.

Loss Soup

❧

FIGURE 1A: THE DINING HALL. Located, it seems, in an abandoned subway tunnel, panelled incongruously in teak, mahogany and other unsustainable hardwoods. Insufficiently lit by dim, recessed lights that give the room an atmosphere of twilight. Walls dustily cluttered with half-completed objects, broken bits of statuary that appear familiar at first glance, and at second glance unrecognisable. Things that make you say to yourself, 'I'll have a closer look at that later,' but, of course, you never do.

FIGURE 1B: THE DINING TABLE. It stretches the length of the hall and appears to be constructed from railway sleepers, or planks from some old galleon. It must weigh many tonnes. Glancing beneath, you see it is supported by a forest of legs of different shapes and sizes, cannibalised from tables, chairs, pedestals, crutches, walking sticks. Laid out upon the bare expanse of wood are two rows of dusty glasses, two rows of earthenware bowls and some wooden spoons.

FIGURE 1C: THE DINERS. At first you assume there are scores of them, but later adjust your estimate to just a few dozen. Calculating numbers is tricky, due to the insufficiency of light and the peculiar amorphousness of facial features. Various races are represented here and there's an equal ratio of women to men, but around this table they all appear generic. It's not helped by the fact they keep changing position without you noticing them move. You turn away from the man to your left, a Slavic gentleman with impressive moustaches, and when you turn back it's an old Asian lady with spectacles like the lenses from antique telescopes. But it's hard to be sure. Your concentration keeps slipping. Perhaps this is still the same person, with a different facial expression.

17

FIGURE 2: THE EGG-TIMER (A). It stands at the furthest end of the table, about the height of a grandfather clock, a truly impressive object. A baroque monstrosity of piped and fluted metal, like something from the palace of the tsars. The dirty golden sand hisses from the top chamber to the bottom, and an ingenious pivoting mechanism allows the whole thing to be rotated when the bottom chamber is full. This task, you imagine, will be performed by the diners sitting on either side, who are watching the sand's flow closely. But the top chamber isn't empty yet.

FIGURE 3A: THE SOUP TUREEN. It is wheeled in on a serving trolley and lifted onto the table by three waiters. Its arrival elicits little excitement from the assembled diners, though you, a first-timer, are awed by its size. 'Could fit a whole lot of soup in there', you scribble on the first page of your notebook. But the tureen, as far as you see, has yet to be filled.

FIGURE 3B: THE LADLE. It's a big one.

FIGURE 4: THE OBSERVER. This is you. You still can't quite believe you've been chosen to attend the fabled Dinner of Loss, but here you sit, notebook on table, wooden spoon in hand. A poorly accredited freelance journalist with a vague interest in 'disappearing things' – you've written articles on language extinction, vanishing glaciers, memory loss – you received the invitation three days ago, and cancelled all other engagements.

You've heard mention of the Dinner of Loss in the course of your research, of course, but doubted if the rumours were true. As far as you know, one lucky observer is invited to attend every year, but you can't imagine how the organisers came to choose you.

You came here in an ordinary taxi, though half expecting to be blindfolded and spun around for disorientation. You entered through an ordinary door, following the instructions. You descended several flights of stairs, walked down a mothball-smelling corridor, entered the long dining hall, and found your place-name waiting.

You've been here about forty-five minutes. The dinner is due to begin.

FIGURE 5: THE GONG. It gongs. Silence settles around the table.

FIGURE 6: THE FIRST INTONATIONS. Delivered by one diner after another, passing around the table in turn, at a steady metronomic pace, in an anticlockwise direction. Running, as far as you can note, as follows:

The auroch. The thylacine. The Barbary lion. The Japanese wolf. The giant short-faced bear. The upland moa. The broad-faced potoroo. The American lion. The elephant bird. The Caucasian wisent. The Yangtze River dolphin. The cave bear. The Nendo tube-nosed fruit bat. The Darling Downs hopping mouse. The Flores dwarf elephant. The Syrian wild ass. The St. Lucy giant rice rat…

You scribble as fast as your pencil can go, but the separately spoken intonations dissolve into a cacophony, murmuring like a disturbed sea, with little rhyme or rhythm. They don't appear to follow any order, whether categorical or chronological. Your writing degrades into improvised shorthand you're not even sure you'll be able to read.

The ground sloth. The pig-footed bandicoot. The Balearic shrew. The Steller's sea cow. The Ilin Island cloudrunner. The Schomburgk's deer. The sea mink. The Javan tiger. The tarpan. The great auk. The Alaotra grebe. The Bermuda night heron. The laughing owl. The bluebuck. The quagga. The western black rhinoceros. The Sturdee's pipistrelle. The turquoise-throated puffleg…

At last the intonations stop. Page after page of your notebook is covered in frenetic scrawls. You think perhaps an hour has passed, but since they removed your watch at the door you have no way of knowing. The only indicator of time is the giant egg-timer down the table, the snakey sand still hissing inside, though the top chamber still isn't empty. Your writing hand throbs painfully, and you're glad of the few minutes' interregnum in which each diner finds their glass has been filled with wine at some point during the proceedings. Following the lead of the other diners, you raise your glass into the air, casting wobbling wine-shadows over the wood.

'Lost animals,' a voice concludes quietly. And as the glasses chime together, the trio of waiters re-enters the hall bearing a steaming vat.

FIGURE 7: LOSS SOUP (A). The waiters approach the soup tureen. You rise from your chair to get a better look, thrilled to be witness to the fabled soup itself, and a slight tut-tut of disapproval issues from the diners beside you. You disregard this. You're a journalist. You can't help but elicit disapproval at times. You lean across the table on tiptoes to get closer to the action.

Actually, there isn't much to see. The waiters remove the tureen's heavy lid and upend the vat. You strain to get a good look at the soup as it sloppily cascades into the tureen, but all you can make out is a viscous gruel, thickened occasionally with matter you can't from this distance identify, a greasy sludge of no definable colour. Although the vat is of no small proportions, you guess the soup that has been poured must cover only an inch or two at the base of the vast tureen. When the gush comes to an end the waiters shake the last drops out, replace the cumbersome china lid, bow to no one in particular, and retire.

FIGURE 8: THE SECOND INTONATIONS. Before you are even resettled in your seat, the next round has begun.

> *Nagumi. Kw'adza. Eyak. Esselen. Island Chumash. Hittite. Eel River Athabaskan. Lycian. Kalkatungu. Moabite. Coptic. Oti. Karipuna. Totoro. Ancient Nubian. Yahuna. Wasu. Apalachee. Old Tatar. Skepi Creole Dutch...*

You begin to feel a little light-headed. Your pencil loses track. You are forced to resort to abbreviations you despair of ever deciphering. But still, you must attempt to keep pace with the murmuring litany of names, must record as many as you can, for they are fast disappearing.

The air itself seems to draw them in. They have no body, no substance. The sounds are like vapour, amorphous, removed from reality.

> *Akkala Sámi. Old Church Slavonic. Bo. Scythian. Cuman. Pictish. Wilson River Karnic. Etruscan. Wagaya-Warluwaric. Edomite. Tangut. Ammonite. Minaean. Phoenician. Ugaritic. Basque-Icelandic pidgin...*

'Lost languages,' the soft voice says, dropping at last a tangible sound – if there can exist such a thing – into a silence you hadn't been made aware of. Glasses clink. You have missed the toast. You are still trying to scribble last names before the sounds go out of your head. But it's no good, you can't remember.

FIGURE 9: LOSS SOUP (B). Again the waiters bring the vat, and you get to your feet to see the gruel slide like an oil slick into the tureen, billowing up clouds of steam. It gives a thin, faintly saline smell. The lid is replaced. The table settles down. The sand inside the egg-timer whispers in the corner.

FIGURE 10: THE THIRD INTONATIONS.

> *The Fijian weinmannia. The Skottsberg's wikstroemia. The Prony Bay xanthostemon. The Maui ruta tree. The root-spine palm. The Franklin tree. The Cuban erythroxylum. The fuzzyflower cyrtandra. The Szaferi birch. The Cuban holly. The Hastings County neomacounia. The toromiro. The Mason River myrtle…*

'Lost plants and trees,' says the voice, and you have the sensation of a door being softly closed, a latch slipping down inside. Again, you weren't aware the litany had ended. Your pencil moves across the table, overshooting its mark. It occurs to you that much time has passed. You were lost in the murmuration, and when you skip back over the pages you find that your notebook is almost full. Hurriedly you fumble in your journalist's pouch in search of a replacement. Glasses clink mildly around the table. You have missed the toast again. The waiters bring the vat.

FIGURE 11: LOSS SOUP (C). The giant tureen still echoes emptily as the soup crashes into the china depths. It looks as if an ocean could slide in there. The oily smell rises unpleasantly, saturating the air around. The smell makes you uncomfortable. It's better to breathe through your mouth.

FIGURE 12: THE FOURTH INTONATIONS.

> *The arctops. The sycosaurus. The gorgonops. The broomisaurus. The eoarctops. The cephalicustriodus. The dinogorgon. The leontocephalus. The inostrancevia. The viatkogorgon…*

'Gorgonopsia,' says the voice. You don't even know what this word means. You check the egg-timer timidly, shaking the cramp from your pencil-clawed hand, but the sand is still flowing down, a never-ending stream.

FIGURE 13: LOSS SOUP (D). Another greyish slurry emits from the vat, frothing as it hits the china walls. You notice some of the diners' mouths are shielded with handkerchiefs. The stink is becoming immense.

FIGURE 14: THE FIFTH INTONATIONS.

> *The Karankawa. The Timucua. The Anasazi. The Thraco-Cimmerians. The Lusatians. The Khazars. The Kipchaks. The Great Zimbabweans. The Olmecs. The Hittites. The Babylonians. The Picts. The Guanches. The Fir Chera. The Gauls. The Tasmanian Aborigines. The Sumerians. The Carthaginians. The Calusa. The Taino. The Mahicans. The Cahokia. The Belgae. The Brigantes. The Ui Liathain. The Thracians. The Kushans. The Amalekites. The Atakapas. The Dzunghars. The Harappans. The Mughals. The Pandyans. The Nazcans. The Seljuks. The Huari. The Chachapoya…*

You find yourself filled with a sense of despair. There appears no meaning behind these names. There is nothing to clutch onto here, they scarcely seem worth the breath they're spoken with. You halt your hopeless scribbling – already you have skipped dozens, scores, perhaps hundreds have not been committed to paper, you will never recall them now – and scan instead the line of faces seated around the dining table, fully and pointlessly intoning. They have no features, no identifying markings. They have reverted to a monotype. Ethnically, sexually and culturally dilute. It's as if every race in the world has been boiled down to its component paste and stirred together into a beige-coloured blandness.

In increasing desperation you search for something, anything. Some clue as to who these people are, or more importantly why they care. But do they care? Why are they here? You try to remember what you have heard in the past about the Dinner of Loss, but find even this has slipped away. What is this roll call supposed to be for? What are you meant to be observing?

You close your notebook, and then your eyes. You'd like to close your nose as well, but the reek of the soup is all-pervading, it's already inside your skin.

FIGURE 15A: THE EGG-TIMER (B). The silence is more general than before, and it takes you a while to understand why. The sand. The sand has finally stopped. You open your eyes and see that the diners have turned their heads to the far end of the hall, where, sure enough, the top chamber stands empty. The bottom chamber is full.

FIGURE 15B: THE EGG-TIMER (C). More servants appear and commence an operation that involves a set of tiny keys, which they use to loosen the brackets that hold the thing together. You realise the entire egg-timer unscrews to divide the top from the bottom chamber. The empty top chamber is leant against the wall, while it takes six men to carry the bottom, staggering towards the dining table with the sand-filled glass bell.

Somehow they lift it onto the table and then clamber onto the table themselves, dragging it over to the tureen. Amid much grunting and strenuous groans the sand is poured into the soup, every last grain shaken out of the chamber. Then the concoction is thoroughly stirred with the oversized ladle.

The pungency of the odour mounts. The diners are gagging politely. You pull your sweater over your face and try not to breathe it in.

Finally the servants do the rounds, ladling soup into each wooden bowl.

'Ladies and gentleman, loss soup,' says the voice, with infinite sadness.

FIGURE 16: LOSS SOUP (E). You stare in some horror at what lies before you. It reeks of bilges, dishwater. An oily film slides on its surface, and when you poke it with the spoon you disturb partially suspended bands of sallow browns and greys. Occasionally a translucent lump of matter rises to the surface, slowly revolves, and then sinks back into the anonymous slop. The sand forms a silt at the bottom of the bowl, something like Turkish coffee.

You cannot remember what you expected, but surely it was something better than this. Perhaps you imagined them swimming down there – shades of the Kipchaks, the wisents, the grebes, the canopies of long-extinct trees, the auroch and the Neanderthal, the glaciers, the megafauna – but you find yourself confronted instead with a sewer-stinking broth. There's not even any wine left to wash the stuff down. Is this perhaps some awful joke?

You look around. The diners are eating, ferrying the soup from their bowls to their mouths with mute determination. The liquid dribbles from their loose lips, splashing back into the bowls. Apart from the pitter-patter of soup drops, the only sound around the table is the steady champing of teeth against sand. Throat muscles clench and gulp. They are actually swallowing the stuff.

As unlikely as it seems, you find yourself incredibly hungry. You feel as if you haven't eaten for weeks. You've lost track of how long you've been in this place. Your stomach aches with emptiness, a hunger of bottomless proportions. Steeling your nerves, you take a spoonful and bring it towards your mouth. But something tells you that would only make it worse. You just can't do it. An enormous sadness billows inside you. Your spoon tips and the soup splashes onto the open page of your notebook, soaking through the paper and blotting the words.

You put the notebook back in its pouch and rise weakly to your feet.

'I'd like… I'd like to add my own,' you say, holding up your empty glass. Hollow eyes swivel but no one speaks. 'My contribution… such as it is. I lost my dad. I mean, we don't speak. We barely know each other these days. And years ago I lost a toy that didn't mean much to anyone else, but to me it was the only thing that seemed at all important. Small Ted. Under a tree in some woods. I used to think about him getting rained on. And… I lost my friends. One in particular. He just went away. Even if he comes back, we're not the same people now. And I lost a love that I needn't have lost. I could have held on but I just didn't try. Now all I remember of her is literally about three things. Something she laughed at once in the bath. That time in a campsite when it hailed. And… I've forgotten certain smells and ideas. What the light was like at this or that moment, things I thought I could never forget… Someone's face, that person's name… Who I was before…'

The words trail off. You've lost yourself now. Something tugs at the back of your mind and for a moment you almost know what it is, but then it disappears like everything else. You sit back in your seat.

The diners stare at you gloomily. Their jaws continue working up and down. The only sound is the sound of champing sand.

Finally you bring the soup to your lips. It doesn't taste of anything at all.

The Golden Age

❧

O nce, having been drunk for a week with his crew aboard the *Queen Anne's Revenge*, it's related that the legendary pirate Blackbeard filled the ship's hold with pots of brimstone, blockaded himself and his men inside, and set the pots aflame. 'Come!' he had cried when this inspiration struck – a slurred debate being waged on deck about the torments they might face in hell – 'let us make a hell of our own, and try how long we can bear it!' The hold filled with noxious smoke and the men retched amid the fumes. Before long they threw the hatches open and burst, gagging, into the light. But Blackbeard stood tall. His mouth clenched. Perspiration bucketed from beneath his tricorn hat. When, at last, he emerged from below – sulphur steaming off his fine clothes, eponymous beard frizzled – he berated his crew for their cowardice with the eloquent words of contempt: 'Damn ye, ye yellow-bellied sapsuckers! I'm a better man than all ye milksops put together!'

It's also told that, in the Gulf of Mexico, he paid homage to the notorious Aztec technique of executing captured conquistadors by pouring molten gold down their throats. His captives were three haughty Spaniards, plantation owners on Hispaniola, whose eyes widened in amazement and terror as the famed buccaneer stoked up a furnace, tossing in the doubloons he had discovered hidden in sacks of sugar. The gold softened, sliding into liquid form like butter in a pan. Into this murderous golden soup Blackbeard dipped a galley ladle, extending it in offering to the first Spaniard's gibbering lips. The poor man wet himself in fear while the crewmen howled with laughter. But instead of forcing the gold down his gullet, Blackbeard spat the following words: 'Ye pap-faced whelp of the Vatican whore – I'll teach ye to wet yeself on my ship! I'll show ye how real men pass water!' And then, to the Spaniards' redoubled amazement, and even greater terror, he gulped the molten metal down himself. Having smacked his lips and wiped his mouth, he pulled down his grubby red breeches, revealing his formidable cock before pissing a fountain of liquid gold all over his captives' shoes.

'Or was it: "I'll teach ye to dirty my boat, ye Cadiz galley-scum"? No, not that. "Ye mollycoddled fondler of boys"? No, it wasn't that neither.' He ponders this now, old Blackbeard, tugging thoughtfully at a kinked strand of hair which is grey now, namesake no longer. '"Ye gaylord"? "Ye shit-heart"? "Ye milk-mouthed suckler of the Virgin Mary's tit"? Ah, it's been too long. I've cursed so many...'

He sits with his slippered feet on a chair, drinking lemonade through a straw. He wears his ancient captain's coat which drapes his thin body like an army blanket, faded tassels of gold brocade hanging from the shoulders. He wears tracksuit bottoms and a knitted scarf wrapped several times around his neck. On his head sits an orange baseball cap.

Blackbeard's ears are full of holes from rings that have long since been lost. If he were to stand against the sky and tug his ears outwards from his head – in order, say, to frighten a child – you'd see daylight shining through. His skin has a taughtened, blasted aspect, the legacy of a lifetime's exposure to salt spray and sun. His body is covered in washed-out tattoos, and a thin scar runs all the way around his sagging, chicken-flesh neck.

The old buccaneer's scraggy grey beard trails down past his waist. In places the beard is plaited and pig-tailed, or dreadlocked with neglect. But in other places – around his mouth – the hair is fastidiously combed.

In recent weeks, he has been discovering unexpected items in his beard. Often there are leaves and twigs after he comes back from a walk, but also broken bits of shell and twists of orange string, polystyrene packaging noodles and ring-pulls from Coca-Cola cans. These findings vaguely worry him. He cannot account for them.

It is documented in the annals of piracy that before Blackbeard went into battle he would light candlesticks in his beard – some say flaming wicks of hemp – to strike fear into his enemies. To a superstitious sailor, press-ganged from the tavern of some West Country fishing village, the sight of this smouldering apparition leering through the powder smoke was often enough to convince them to surrender without discharging a shot. What is not so commonly known is that, in his wilder moments, Blackbeard would stuff his mouth with fireworks and spew out magnesium flares. In one fight, he dipped his entire head in pitch and set fire to his face, charging aboard a Royal Navy flagship with no fewer than eleven swords of different shapes and sizes. It is reported that, in this notable attack, one officer was so petrified that he committed suicide.

Blackbeard is eating cauliflower cheese and looking out of the window. 'Can ye bring me the sauce?' he calls over his shoulder, getting cheese on the tips of his moustache. His daughter Jess puts the ketchup on the table, rests her hand briefly on his shoulder. She brushes some specks of dirt from the epaulettes, wondering how he manages to get his shoulders dirty.

'How's the food?' she asks.

'Thank ye, just the way I likes it.'

'I'm off to the gallery now,' she says, picking a set of keys from the fruit bowl, her mobile phone from the table. 'You'll be alright this afternoon?'

'Aye, just fine,' says Blackbeard, squinting at his daughter. Jess's skin gives a soft glow, diffusing like the light from a lantern. By contrast her dark hair seems to draw the light back in. Her lips are the colour of pecan nuts. She is wearing faded jeans and a muslin blouse, a necklace of cowrie shells. She is even more beautiful than her mother was. But he cannot think about that.

She starts to tell him about the week ahead, preparing for the exhibition. The tourist season is approaching, and the gallery has agreed to display some of her work in the window. She has a studio in the old boatshed that stands behind the house, and here she carves figurines from sea-sculpted driftwood, using the wood's natural warp and flow to fashion animals, human forms. Her father brings her wood from the beach, if he happens to remember.

'What are you smiling at?' she asks, seeing he has not listened.

'Ah… it's nothing, Jessy,' he says.

But Blackbeard is thinking back to another meal. His eyes are not seeing the table. He is back beneath the swishing palms, the dark waves lapping at the edges of the reef. There are wild pigs crackling over the fire, swordfish baked in banana leaves, rum poured from green coconuts. He feasts in a circle of thirty men – white men, black men, yellow men, men who have lost all nationality – slurping conch soup from a turtle shell, tearing pork off a glistening bone. He is shooting pistol shots at the moon, leaping barefoot over flames. One pirate reenacts the battle with a monkey, shrieking as the monkey beats him with a spoon. A fat buccaneer with bejewelled teeth sets fire to a captured Royal Navy ensign, and Blackbeard applauds as the flag goes up, roars out a mock national anthem.

'Dad? I'm off.'

'Alright then, Jessy.'

'I'll be back around eight.' She pauses. 'What are you laughing about?'

'Ah, just thinking o' some old joke. Before ye was born,' he says.

He is lying on the cool sand, two crewmen pouring rum into his mouth. He is making a speech with no trousers on. Dancing a waltz with a shin bone. Sipping French wine from the polished skull of the Admiralty bitch, Lieutenant Maynard!

⚓

Blackbeard progresses to the harbour now, descending a street that has been re-cobbled recently with national lottery money. He passes pubs with fishing nets arranged in their windows, framed displays of different examples of knot. He follows a row of trinket shops that sell souvenirs from the sea – shell earrings, seahorses, shark-tooth pendants – as well as plastic pistols and cutlasses, Jolly Roger flags, felt tricorn hats. At a shop called Maritime Days he stops to study the hats through the glass.

'Is that one mine? Did it look like that? I never had one of those.'

In the window near the novelty hats is a selection of false moustaches and beards. The grandest, a luxuriant nest of silky, black synthetic hair, bears the label: 'Blackbeard's Beard!' The old man stares, aghast for a moment, then puts his fingers to his facial hair and tugs it doubtfully. It does not come away in his hand.

'That's something, anyway. At least there's that.' He wanders on, confused.

In the Paper Moon Tea Rooms, down by the quay, he meets his old friend and shipmate Cut Hands Jim. Cut Hands is eating toast and marmalade, topping up his pot of Darjeeling with gin. Blackbeard takes a seat at his table, studies the red and white checkered cloth.

'Good day, young Edward,' says Cut Hands with his mouth full. It is not known why, but he has always called Blackbeard by his Christian name, Edward Teach.

'Hello, Cut Hands.'

'Do ye want some toast?'

'No thank ye, Cut Hands. I'm not hungry.'

The two friends sit in silence for a while. The waitress, an observant Polish girl, brings Blackbeard his usual lemon and ginger tea with a small pot of honey on the side. He pours the honey carefully, watching it slide off the tip of the spoon, then stirs the tea into a whirlpool and breathes deeply through his large nose.

'Liquid gold,' he murmurs. 'Ye Cadiz galley-scum...'

'What's that, Edward?'

'Them were the days.'

'Aye,' nods Cut Hands vaguely. 'Them were indeed the days.' Blackbeard smiles wordlessly, cradling his cup close to his face so the steam curls up around his chin.

Cut Hands has a wooden leg. Every so often, with great satisfaction, Blackbeard leans back and has a peek under the table to remind himself. A hardwood peg with a rubber tip, notched where he has banged it into things.

Cut Hands also has a shiny bald head, peeling a little from the sun. He wears a yellow and green striped shirt and a pair of corduroy trousers. On the back of his left hand, resting on the table, can be seen a faint blue smudge which was once the outline of a heart transfixed by a spear.

Blackbeard watches Cut Hands's hand and sees it holding fast on the helm. The sleeve rolled back, the muscled forearm glistening with spray. He hears the fluttering of a flag, the creak of oily ropes.

'Mild today,' says Cut Hands, tweaking at the lace curtain. A band of watery sunlight slides across the table.

'Pressure could drop awful sudden, though,' suggests Blackbeard hopefully. 'Ye know how them squalls blow in...'

'No. Be mild all week, I think.' Cut Hands slurps his tea.

As attested by contemporary observers – whether victims of his piracy or allies who sailed with him – the standard that flew above Blackbeard's ships depicted a horned skeleton, holding an egg-timer in one hand and using the other to jab a spear towards a red heart with three drops of blood falling from it. Blackbeard is said to have designed it himself, after rejecting submissions from his crew which included, among other things, a mermaid with enormous breasts and a flaming sheep skull for a face, a hanged man kicking an angel in the balls, and an octopus strangling a bishop. The flag was first hoisted on the *Queen Anne's Revenge* before her famous attack on the *Scarborough*, a British thirty-gun man-of-war, the audacity of which propelled Blackbeard into transatlantic fame.

The meaning of the flag is clear: that time is running out for whoever is unfortunate enough to behold it, that the skeleton must be appeased, or blood will surely follow. And yet, to pirate enthusiasts accustomed to grinning Jolly Roger flags, the image appears oddly bathetic. The skeleton's rickety legs and protruding hip bones make it look as if it suffers from a degenerative bone disease. And the expression on its skull face is not the expected devilish glee, but a kind of mournful uncertainty, as if no quantity of blood will console its sadness.

'But it struck terror into their hearts. Did it not, Cut Hands?'

'Whose hearts, Edward?'

'Ye know whose hearts! Ye know true well.' Blackbeard covers his mouth with his hand, as if he is about to sneeze. A chortling sound issues from between his fingers. 'Do ye remember the Charleston Blockade?'

'Course I do, Ed. Everyone remembers.'

'How them dolled-up gumbo-suckers grovelled, down on their knees? Snivelling like babies! We ransomed the entire town, penned 'em in their poxy harbour for a fortnight. Hah! Or were it a month?'

'I think it were a week. Far as I can recall.' Cut Hands rubs his head, causing folds of skin to ripple from his eyebrows to his crown. 'How's ye're girl?' he asks after a pause. 'I heard she's got some kind o' show...'

But Blackbeard's eyes are like coins. He sees magistrates in powdered wigs, admirals who once had commanded fleets, French aristocrats in satin and ridiculous pomades. And that cretinous, cowardly wretch Lieutenant Maynard – dancing a pretty jig across the deck while cutlass strokes sang past his ears!

According to reliable reports, one of Blackbeard's favourite tactics involved hurling burning rats aboard the ships of his opponents. He would dip them in buckets of pitch by their tails, then sprinkle them with gunpowder. A fine sight, to see them trailing sparks as they soared in flaming arcs across the sky towards the delicate rigging of an unsuspecting sloop. They used to hold contests for good aim. He once hit a cabin-boy smack in the eye.

'Like comets, they was... fiery angels o' death. No one else did it like we did, Cut Hands. No one else even came close.'

Not with the same bright bubbling joy, the same vicious happiness.

The feeling comes back to him in starts, rising through his chest and face, heating him, making him dizzy. Had anyone else ever known these things? Had anyone truly lived? It had not been unknown for him to drink three whole barrels of rum, and after one especially lucrative raid he reportedly married thirteen different women in one night.

That was before Jess's mother, of course. But he cannot think about that.

'And ye must remember the time, I think it were off St Kitts, when we fired ye from a cannon?' Blackbeard's face balls up with mirth. Blackbeard's shoulders tremble. 'Ye tore a hole through the topsail o' a Dutchy merchantman, and then ye slew twenty sailors with an axe. By the time the *Revenge* caught ye up, ye was already mopping the decks!'

'I don't think so, Ed. No, I never did that.'

'Come now, ye must remember. That's how ye lost ye're hair, after all.'

'I just went bald. Like other men.'

'Ye're leg, then! That's how ye lost ye're leg!'

'Edward,' says Cut Hands kindly.

The waitress comes to remove some plates from the table next to theirs. There is no one else in the Paper Moon Tea Rooms. She smiles at the two old men, understanding little of what they say. She knows that the gentle bald one smuggles gin into his tea, but as long as the owner isn't around she chooses not to notice.

'He steered us safe through a hurricane, once,' Blackbeard mumbles, half to her and half to himself, motioning with his teaspoon. 'He were the best helmsman on the *Revenge*. The best man in my fleet…'

And now he is thinking of that sandy inlet, the coastal waters of North Carolina. The place that was to be known as Teach's Hole.

Fighting side by side on the HMS *Ranger*, slicing and gouging through the pistol smoke, Maynard's men having ambushed them from their hiding place in the hold.

Laughing as he deflected bullets with his sword. Breaking two sailors' necks with his knee. Neatly lopping off a leg to wield as a weapon.

The intervening years have swallowed so much. Things have drifted from view, become lost. Blackbeard struggles to maintain his hold, clinging against the entropic trends, but somehow little things get swept away. History, for example, has neglected to remember how he swung into battle naked from a rope, his body covered in barnacles, or dived underneath an enemy ship to hack open its keel with a billhook. The official record only informs that he was tricked into attacking, outmanoeuvered and outgunned at Ocracoke Island, North Carolina – that he'd been drinking heavily in his cabin the night before, and attempted to board the hostile vessel with only a handful of men – that he was shot five times, and stabbed more than twenty. But the records do not document how the cutlass blades simply glanced off his bones, or how he retched the bullets into his mouth and spat them right back at the cowards who had fired them, plugging the holes in his perforated stomach with corks from brandy bottles…

Rising from the ocean like a vengeful Poseidon with seawater sluicing from his beard, catching that miserable Maynard by the ankle to drag him down, into the deepening blue…

'He wasn't no match for me, Cut Hands. Not for the King o' Pirates! That shit-heart… bilge-scum… Admiralty whore…' The epithets descend into mutters that lose themselves in his beard.

'But Lieutenant Maynard cut ye're head off, Ed,' says Cut Hands quietly. 'Chopped it off and hung it from the bowsprit, he did. They gave him a hundred pounds.'

Blackbeard is silent. He sits without moving. Down into the deepening blue…

'And that was the end o' the Golden Age. The end o' the innocent days.' Cut Hands shuffles his feet beneath the table. His wooden leg is just a walking stick, tipped with a rubber stopper. He is wearing a pair of frayed rope sandals from a beachwear store on the high street.

Blackbeard chews the inside of his lip. Closes his tired eyes. The inside of his head is the colour of waves sloshing back on themselves against a quay, a pale bottle-green interspersed with fine bubbles. He finds himself thinking of oranges, driftwood. An egg-timer and three drops of blood. The ring-pulls from Coca-Cola cans. He cannot account for these things.

'But don't ye recall what happened then, Ed?' Cut Hands sees the tears welling up, and he cannot stand to see that. 'Don't ye remember what ye did next? Those Navy dogs tossed ye're body overboard – and ye're headless corpse, it swam three times around the *Queen Anne's Revenge*!'

'Seven! Seven times, it were!' cries Blackbeard happily.

'Aye, seven. It were seven times,' says Cut Hands, taking his last bite of toast. 'That shitted them up a treat.'

Blackbeard is walking along the beach, following the tideline westwards. The sand is a sloppy mirror at his feet. The salty wind makes his eyeballs sting. He finds it hard to see.

From habit, he scans the brackish waste that the water has ploughed into decomposing rows. The piled seaweed is almost black, hopping with tiny flies. Kicking his way through the stinking wrack he uncovers a child's plastic shoe, tangles of orange nylon rope, part of a broken crate from a Spanish trawler. He fills his pockets with this and that, collects colourful bottle-caps. Tugs out a sea-smoothed lump of driftwood that looks a bit like a monkey, or a child, and carries it for a while.

'I'll take this back for Jessy,' he says. But later he puts it down on a rock and wanders on, forgetting.

On his way home he stops at Maritime Days, glimpsing the pretty ship-in-a-bottle in the window. Counting out the loose coins from his pocket, he doesn't have quite enough for it, but the shop assistant knows the old sailor and lets him owe a pound or two. At the top of the hill he regards it admiringly – the matchstick mast, the rigging made of thread – turning it around in his thick fingers.

The ocean heaves. The storm is at hand. Blackbeard holds fast on the helm, laughing into the wind and the rain, steadily driving his good ship westwards, into the hurricane.

The Horse Latitudes

❧

The ocean is white and pink and purple and red and yellow and brown and green. After weeks at sea, the captain clambers up the mast of his yacht and scans the horizon with binoculars, rotating himself degree by degree until he has turned full circle. 'This is it. I am here.'

There are nothing but plastic bottles, plastic bottles as far as he can see.

The yacht slides on, carving a V-shaped wake through the bottles as it goes. The captain turns to watch the gash – brief glimpses of a dirty blue – slowly filling in behind, erasing all traces of his passing.

He hugs the mast and shuts his eyes. He feels nothing, not even the wind.

The bottles clunk gently against one another, so softly he can hardly hear them.

Down on deck, he opens the freezer and takes out a miniature bottle of champagne. He pours the champagne into a plastic cup, which he raises towards the sky. He pauses, frowning, and thinks for a while.

'Yes, this is it,' he says finally. 'Yes, I am here.'

He drinks the champagne in tiny sips, gazing at the bottle-covered ocean.

All the colours in the world are there, worn dull by the waves.

When the last drop of champagne is gone, he tosses the bottle overboard. Then he tosses the cup over too. Within seconds he can no longer see them.

The yacht drifts on for an hour. Half a day. The ocean's surface changes. The plastic bottles become interspersed with other items of debris: footballs, tangled carrier bags, crumbled hunks of polystyrene, flip-flops, bergs of packaging foam. The captain watches it slip by with a sense of awe. He spots flower pots, fragments of fishing crates, once the half-submerged torso of a doll. He wonders if the head is here too, and if so, whether the motion of the waves will ever push them back together.

The yacht drifts on. Its prow cuts a swathe through Tupperware boxes, lids, foil wrapping, crisp packets, objects he can't identify. Always plastic bottles, in their hundreds and thousands. He squints overboard to read the names, or recognises brands from faded blocks of colour: Coca-Cola, Pepsi, 7-Up, Schweppes, Sunkist, Mountain Dew.

Occasionally something larger bumps against the hull: half a green plastic garden chair, a refrigerator door. They could have come from anywhere, from any land in the world.

Later, the captain goes below and heats a ready-meal in the microwave. He eats chicken chow mein from a greasy plastic tub, and, after wiping it clean, tosses the tub over the side, along with its plastic fork.

The tub drops between an empty ice-cream carton, so faded he cannot make out the name, and a four-litre bottle that once contained mineral water.

How quickly things return to their own. It satisfies him, somehow.

Night falls over the plastic sea. The captain wraps up warm and sits on deck, watching the sunset with a bottle of wine and a packet of cigarettes. The ocean is calm, its gentle undulations spreading slow ripples through the trash, giving it almost the effect of breathing. The falling sun catches on pieces of foil and shards of bright PVC. Gradually all colour leaches from the scene, leaving only spots of white that appear to glow as if holding the light, as everything else goes dark.

Alone on his yacht, it seems to the captain as if he's never seen anything so lovely.

The horse latitudes are situated between thirty and thirty-five degrees on both sides of the equator. Wind and rain are uncommon there. The ocean is subdued. The captain has always enjoyed the name as much as the legend from which it sprung: that Spanish ships, becalmed for weeks on the glassy millpond sea, would be forced to throw their horses overboard when water supplies ran low.

Of course, it's a dubious theory. But the name is apt. In the days before plastic was conceived of, the captain imagines an ocean of abandoned

horses, bobbing gently up and down, their hooves sticking up towards the sky.

The North Pacific Gyre, through which the northern horse latitude runs, is located in the Pacific Ocean between the equator and fifty degrees north. A gyre is a vortex caused by a system of rotating ocean currents; in the case of the North Pacific, the currents that turn this vast wheel of water are the North Pacific Current, the California Current, the North Equatorial Current and the Kuroshio Current, which between them spin the ocean in a clockwise direction, channelling debris to a central point from which it cannot escape.

The existence of the rubbish patch through which the captain is drifting now – wrapped up in his sleeping-bag, one arm dangling over the bunk, dreaming of nothing that he will recall – was theorised before it was observed. Researchers studying oceanic currents predicted such an effect. It wasn't until the closing years of the garbage-strewn twentieth century that a sailing ship, cutting through the subtropical high between Hawai'i and California, entered an uncharted ocean of plastic that took a full week to traverse.

The area's true size is unknown. Estimates range from three hundred thousand to almost six million square miles.

It seems unbelievable, in an age of aeroplanes and satellites, that such a vast region of pollution could have remained unseen for so long. But these are seas seldom travelled. They lie thousands of miles from the nearest landmass, their emptiness unbroken by islands. They lie on no trade routes, shipping lanes or notable fishing grounds. This is an ocean en route to nowhere. A convenient vanishing zone for lost, unwanted things.

Also, all is not visible, not to the naked eye. There's more to the patch than rafts of Pepsi bottles and atolls of Styrofoam. Mostly it consists of particles that have been ground by the action of the waves to a minute, multicoloured sand, partially suspended below the surface, in the upper neustonic and epipelagic layers of the water column. Plastic cannot biodegrade. Its tightly bound polymers cannot unravel. It can only reduce and reduce, growing tinier with each passing year, from the miniscule to the molecular level, changing the composition of the sea.

Humankind's first plastic, celluloid, was invented in 1855. The first entirely synthetic plastic was bakelite, fifty-two years later. This was followed by epoxy, polystyrene and polyvinyl chloride, polyethylene, polytetrafluoroethylene, polypropylene, polycarbonate, polymethyl methacrylate, melamine formaldehyde; nylon, Styrofoam, PVC, Teflon, Plexiglas, Perspex. The products were mated with themselves to develop ever-stronger bonds, polymers that could not be broken; resistant to heat, friction, crystallisation and biodegradation. The twentieth century was the plastic age, when human beings at last tore free from organic strictures.

The captain mumbles the names of the plastics. He recites them to the waves, watching the colours merge and bloom. Surely the very first particles are here, in the centre of the North Pacific Gyre. Ground to a microscopic dust. They have been here for a hundred years, waiting for humankind to catch up.

Going to the centre of the gyre is like travelling back in time. Back to the dead hub of everything, from which nothing can escape.

On his third day in the gyre, the captain sees a boat on the horizon. At first he thinks he is mistaken. But the boat comes closer. It's a curious kind of boat, with a long, sharp prow like a canoe, and two fine grilles extending like wings from its port and starboard sides.

The boat is crewed by two men and a woman wearing red T-shirts displaying the logo of an oceanographic institute.

The captain watches them with amusement as they squint and stare.

'What are you doing?' asks one of the men when they are within talking distance.

'Nothing. What are you doing?' says the captain.

The man explains they have built this vessel as part of an investigation into pelagic plastic pollution in the North Pacific. He says this craft will pioneer a clean-up operation of vast proportions, to be shared between responsible nations, in which hundreds of thousands of tonnes of waste will be skimmed from the ocean's surface.

The captain doesn't say anything. He takes a Dairy Milk bar from his pocket and breaks off a square.

The woman continues from where the man left off. She tells the captain of their studies into the effect of plastic pollution on the surrounding ecosystem and marine wildlife. She opens a freezer-box on the deck and produces a sodden albatross, its throat tangled with nylon fibre, polystyrene wedged in its gullet. In parts of the North Pacific, she says, plastic micro-pellets outnumber zooplankton by a factor of seven. Plastic has crept into the food chain, is being ingested by everything from jellyfish to large mammals. No one yet has the slightest idea of what impact this might have.

The captain watches patiently as the woman displays her other exhibits: a triggerfish with three bottle caps in its belly, a guillemot full of foam.

When the researchers have finished speaking, he eats his last square of Dairy Milk. He lets the wrapper drift away in the breeze, where it comes to rest against a polyethylene milk jug.

The researchers stare at him from their boat.

'Asshole,' says the woman.

'You expect to clean a whole ocean with that?' says the captain, without any malice.

'Come on, let's go,' says the woman. She slams the lid of her albatross box.

'Even if you skim off a thousand tonnes, what will you do with it? Burn it? Bury it in the ground? I don't understand.'

The woman ignores him. She puts on a baseball cap that matches the logo on her red T-shirt.

'How long have you been out here?' calls one of the men as their craft pulls away. 'Where are you headed?'

The captain doesn't answer him, but he shields his eyes to watch the boat go, growing gradually more indistinguishable, and finally raises his hand in a salute.

That evening he smokes three cigarettes and drinks half a bottle of wine. He lies on his back on the deck and watches the daylight disappear. He makes noises, of varying pitches and depths. The stars are brilliant here.

The engine is silent. The sail is furled. The yacht rests, curlicued with foam. The captain spends his days on deck, reading old nautical magazines, observing small changes in the sky, making inventories and counting his rations. One day the rain begins falling lightly, and lasts for an hour or so. It seems to the captain that rain on the ocean is a waste of water.

He doesn't have much need to eat, and he sleeps surprisingly little.

He has seen no other boats. He doesn't expect to see them.

The captain has enough supplies, carefully stacked in the hold, to survive for a couple of years in the gyre. Assuming he eats just one meal a day, assuming he drinks exactly one half-litre bottle of water. The alcohol, chocolate and cigarettes will run out after six months or so, but he hopes that by that point, he won't have need of them.

He has also brought fishing lines, hooks and nets and sinkers. The ocean contains fish of all shapes and sizes, even here, among so much waste. The fish will be saturated with plastic, infinitesimal nurdles. He will ingest vinyl chloride and di-2-ethylhexyl phthalate, carcinogenic and mutagenic, substances banned by responsible nations. In this way, he will enter the food chain. He will arrive at its apex. The plastic sea will pass into him, changing his composition.

But for now he leaves the lines alone. It occurs to him that he packed no bait. He will have to bait his hooks with pieces of chicken chow mein.

It is hard to tell, without instruments, whether the yacht is drifting on the waves or whether the ocean's surface is changing, subtly shifting its patterns. The depths are far too great to drop anchor, but, without wind, he assumes he will simply remain where he is, slowly revolving around the same point. There are no other factors to act upon him. He came here to go nowhere.

He has the image in his mind of the plastic ceaselessly spreading around him, expanding like a summer bloom of algae. Every scrap, every wrapper, every polystyrene coffee cup that finds a route from the land to the sea, from Japan to Mexico, is making its way towards him now, inevitably honing in. He sits at the centre of an orbit, dragging in lost things.

Sometimes, if the captain squints, if he has drunk a bottle of wine, if he has spent the night on deck, making noises at the stars, he sees things in the pattern of the seas. Amorphous pictures that break and blend, dotted masses of colour. Sometimes it looks like grazing flamingos seen from an aeroplane through clouds. Sometimes it looks like thousands of faces, all the races of the world, crowds at a great political rally at which he is centre stage. Sometimes it looks like old film footage, slowly zooming into the grain. Sometimes it looks like a pointillist painting. Meadows of spring flowers.

He has been three months in the North Pacific Gyre. It doesn't feel so long.

He has come to recognise familiar landmarks in the structure of the sea. An island of polyurethane foam. Tangled reefs of purple twine. Archipelagos of bottle caps.

He thinks about the horses long ago, pitched overboard like disposable cups. Bobbing gently up and down, their hooves sticking up towards the sky.

He has a ream of paper on deck and he spends long hours making diagrams, charting the uncharted spaces of the ocean. Inventing names for things unnamed. Making maps of a strange new world.

Cow's Head

❧

When the Karankawa learned my name they fell about with mirth. Their tattooed faces opened up and they howled and hooted. One of the men had a choking fit. Several women seized my beard and tugged upon it painfully. The terrible naked children pranced and made bestial sounds, holding their fingers up like horns, imitating my own imitations of a creature that none of them had ever seen, or even heard about, until myself and my few companions washed up on their stinking shore. The Lord, in His wisdom, had not seen fit to bless that undomesticated breed with useful beasts of the field. Cattle were unknown to them. Still, I tried my best.

'Cabeza de Vaca,' I said again – partly in my native Castilian and partly in the few words I had learned of their unlovely tongue, composed of xs, qs and ks – 'a title bestowed on an illustrious ancestor on my mother's side, referring to his brave actions during the struggle against the Moors…' Over exclamations of amusement I tried to explain about the skull, and the Cliff of Plunging Dogs, and the honour that was won on the bloody field of battle. But the Karankawa did not listen. They wiped tears from their eyes.

'Cow's Head!' they cried, delighted.

Attempting a spirit of forbearance, as befits a Christian, I did my best to ignore their rudeness and focus on higher things. I gazed past the mocking savages who had enslaved and belittled me, past their slovenly huts of sticks and their racks of stinking fish, past my companions in misfortune – the noblemen Andres Dorantes de Carranza and Alonso del Castillo Maldonado and the former slave, himself a Moor, whom we only knew as Estevanico – to the shore that lay beyond. My eyes absorbed the grey sand flats, the snake-infested brackish pools, the labyrinthine tidal channels down which our unfortunate raft had come, the malarial swamps and the sea beyond, whose waves were the colour of chicken fat that has congealed in the sun. The horizon shuddered in the heat and I shuddered with it. Biting flies hung off my arms. That morning I had had to remove a leech from my left testicle.

'Cow's Head!' yelled an insolent girl whose cheeks were pierced with a bone. 'Cow's Head!' laughed an old man, slapping his alligator-oil-smeared thighs.

What slighted me more than anything else was to see Estevanico smile too. He hid his mouth with his hand but I could see it in his eyes. One more humiliation in a lifetime of humiliations.

I took a deep breath, walked away down the beach, and went back to shucking oysters.

The technique was to push a blade into the oyster's gritty hinge and turn it like a key, prising the carapace apart to reveal the wetly gleaming flesh. Push, twist, push, twist. How I loathed the task. At first I had kept count, maintaining a tally in my head, thinking the numbers would come in useful when I wrote my chronicles – along with heights, depths, distances and the other important statistics I was storing in my memory for when the occasion might arise – but somewhere in the low ten thousands I had given up. Push, twist, push, twist. The harvest was unending. The Karankawa had trekked along this coast for weeks to reach this place, at which, I gathered, they enjoyed some ancient ancestral right to gorge themselves on the slimy meat until their bodies reeked. From dawn till dusk they waded in the shallow sea up to their necks and prowled the wetlands in small boats, dredging up sack after sack, and from dawn to dusk we toiled, through the wet heat of the day, in a glistening midden of snapped and shattered shells. It was drudging, thankless work. The men made the women do it and the women made us do it. The only variation came in the form of other types of shellfish – with which the Lord, for reasons of His own, had prodigiously stocked this coast – in the forms of mussels, scallops, clams, conches, limpets, snails, innumerable spiked and plated crabs, shrimps, lobsters, crayfish and other horrid sea-lice. We wrenched off legs, cracked open claws, ripped off smelly brown beards and thumbed out pulsing flesh, almost glad of the diversion until the next appalling sack of oysters crashed at our feet. Push, twist, push, twist. Soon our fingers were as calloused as the shells they handled.

The Karankawa's attitude to slaves was somewhat different from our own. We were not shackled or restrained, and neither were we confined at night. Ostensibly we were free to roam about as we pleased and pass the time in whatever manner we saw fit. But we were weak and feverish, demoralised, absolutely lost, and those members of our party who had attempted an escape had either perished in the swamps – their flyblown bodies sometimes drifting back on the brackish tide, their faces bloated, sad and green – or been killed by the spears and poisoned arrows of neighbouring tribes, with whom the Karankawa maintained a lazy warfare. In this way, and through disease, our numbers had been reduced from almost forty men to four in the six months since we'd arrived, and none of us possessed the will to try to change things now. If we refused to work we received no punishment – no beatings, whippings, brandings or torments of any kind – but seeing as our only food was the shellfish that we shucked, inevitably we toiled on. We did not know what else to do. Perhaps we were not slaves at all; it was never made explicit.

Clammy oysters filled my dreams. Sometimes I was inside the shell, a globule of pale flesh listening in mute terror as someone tapped and scraped my walls, probing for an entrance point. My exposed parts were cruelly scooped into scalding sunlight. At other times I prised apart a shell to reveal, instead of meat, a tiny, perfect cow's head nested like a foetus.

I first arrived in this New World in the year 1527 in the service of Panfilo de Narvaez, a veteran of the conquests of Cuba and Jamaica. We were six hundred men, drawn from every part of Spain, some of whom had fought against the Moors in their younger days, or – as I had myself – participated in the conquest of the Guanches of the Canary Islands, a heathen folk with matted hair who dressed in shaggy sheepskins. Staggered by the wealth that was pouring out of Mexico, which had fallen to Cortes only six years previously, His Majesty King Carlos V had sent us far along the coast to penetrate the unknown interior of La Florida, the mysterious Land of Flowers, in the hope that even greater treasures lay within. We went with God in our hearts and gold and glory in our minds. Our swords were sharp, our armour bright, and our moustaches waxed and curled. Of course I dreamed, like all the rest, of undiscovered empires and cities paved with precious stones, of men who clothed themselves in gold, of emperors throwing wide their gates and falling in supplication at our iron-booted feet. I would return to Spain a wealthy and distinguished man, the banner of my noble family fluttering in the sea-wind.

It did not turn out like that. These things did not happen.

It took the best part of a month to make the crossing from Cuba, a distance of little more than a hundred miles, because of a ferocious current pushing back against us. Our ships kept being blown off course and going round in circles. By the time we made landfall many of our men were sick, and my favourite horse had died and been thrown in the sea. We came ashore at the edge of a vast and sultry jungle – a tangle of buzzing green prowled by naked Indians who stared in blank incomprehension when we asked them about gold – and set up camp in the rain, tormented by mosquitoes. Narvaez, inexplicably, decided to divide our force, leaving three hundred men with the ships and leading the other three hundred inland. I advised against this course, but no one listened to me.

Once the coast was out of sight the heat closed on us like a wall. We could hardly draw breath, let alone march in armour. Nevertheless we ventured on, our horses wading up to their bellies in grey stinking mud, hacking back the greenery with our blades of Toledo steel. Based on the interrogation of some natives he had caught – never mind the minor fact that no one understood their tongue – Narvaez was convinced that a city lay ahead of us, a fabulous place called Apalachee, where we might be fed and feted as guests of its emperor while we planned to conquer it, as Cortes had in Mexico. We reached that place after a month. It consisted of forty houses. We took its ruler prisoner and ransacked its stores of maize – our food supplies were much depleted, having spoiled in the humid air – but almost immediately we found ourselves under siege from a large force of Indians attacking from the forest. They came in alternating shifts, never giving us a moment's peace. In the time it took to load and fire an arquebus they could unleash a dozen arrows and vanish back into the trees. Our corpses looked like pin-cushions. After several days we left, burning down the houses. We fought our way from one godforsaken village to the next, persecuted and pursued, our horses shot from under us, men falling in their droves. Narvaez promoted me to captain but I contracted diarrhoea, which was a great indignity. It is hard to maintain composure, or give sensible commands, when hot shit is bubbling down your inside legs like gravy. All I could do was soldier on and trust in the mercy of the Lord. The cities of gold were out there somewhere; we just had to find them.

After our ill-fated force had lost fully a third of its men, without having found an ounce of gold, Narvaez decided we should go back to the coast. We could not find our original route so wandered vaguely southwards. When at last we staggered from the steaming mass of greenery and saw the white sand, and the surf, there was no sign of our ships. We did not know whether they had left, or whether – as seemed more likely – this was a different stretch of coast, perhaps hundreds of miles off course. Either way: disaster. For a week we despaired, straining our eyes in vain for a glimpse of distant sails, dreading the anticipated hiss and thump of arrows. Then I had an idea. I presented it to Narvaez, who had spent the last few days pacing round and round the beach in a figure-of-eight pattern muttering viciously to himself and occasionally weeping. He immediately pulled himself together and claimed the idea as his own, which angered but did not surprise me. There was no time to dwell on it. He was shouting orders.

The idea was this: we would slaughter our horses, salt their meat, build a furnace out of clay, construct a bellows from deer skin, melt down all the iron we had – horseshoes, stirrups, bridal bits, spurs, the buckles from our belts – forge the iron into nails, use the horsehair to make ropes, and construct five large rafts, each capable of carrying fifty men. Then we would flee that dreadful land by following the coastline west to the safety of His Majesty's imperial province of New Spain, otherwise known as Mexico.

The plan went well, at first.

It saddened us to cut the throats of our faithful, wretched steeds and watch them bleed out on the sand. We named that place the Bay of Horses in their honour. We stoked the fire and watched the iron melt in the crucible, hammered the hot lumps into points, lashed the planks with horsehair ropes. The rafts looked strong and seaworthy. The sky was blue and clear. As we boldly launched ourselves and cleared the surging surf some of us gave thanks to God and others bellowed out sea-songs – in Castilian, Catalan, Basque and all the dialects of Spain – accompanied by obscene gestures at the shrinking coastline.

For weeks we paddled west, chewing horsemeat and watching the land slide past.

At last things were going well. Then came the hurricane.

It raged for days and nights on end. The waves were foaming mountains. One by one the rafts broke apart and their men were lost, scattering out across the sea, thrashing their limbs desperately. Very few of them could swim, and it wouldn't have done them any good. Narvaez sunk like a rock, weighed down by his armour. In the fury of the storm I found myself clinging to Estevanico and heard him scream in Arabic, calling out to his Allah. This might be blasphemous to say, but perhaps it did some good. Our raft remained intact and was carried towards the shore. There were forty of us left. The hurricane abated.

Crawling on the grey sand, too weak to stagger to my feet, I found that my path was blocked by a palisade of slender poles. Then I realised it was not a palisade, but legs. I looked up to find myself surrounded by men and women with intricate, dark tattoos and piercings in their lips and cheeks, their long hair thickly smeared with a kind of pungent grease. They did not look impressed. 'Karankawa,' they said.

Over the next several days they nursed us back to health, feeding us and letting us sleep, dressing our wounds with leaves and a poultice made from boiled frogs. Thirteen of our number died, but I was not among them. Some of the men became convinced that the savages were fattening us up to eat, and made their way one moonless night into the swampland to escape, but – we learned soon enough – they did not get very far. Their bodies were brought back to camp and unceremoniously buried. When we had regained our strength a group of women came for us. They looked rather pleased with themselves. They led myself and the other survivors down the beach to a new location, where, we dimly saw ahead, enormous piles of black stones lay scattered all around. They pointed at the stones and grinned.

Then we saw they were not stones. They were piles of oysters.

Several tens of thousands of shucked shells later, here we were.

'Estevanico,' I said that night, 'I would like to ask you something.'

Andres Dorantes de Carranza and Alonso del Castillo Maldonado were snoring on the sand nearby, twitching with troubled dreams. Myself and the Moor were still awake, burning seaweed to keep the flies away, soaking our hands in salt water to sterilise the lacerations they had received that day in the course of their endless duty.

Estevanico turned to me, his face orange in the firelight.

'Do you think my name comical?' I asked.

His mouth twitched very slightly. He cleared his throat.

I do not know why it was that I sought his opinion in this matter, but the laughter of the Karankawa had strangely wounded me. Painstakingly I had begun to learn their language in order to communicate in something other than gestures and grunts – against the recommendations of my fellow noblemen, who said that a Christian tongue should not so debase itself – until finally I was ready to attempt a formal introduction. Explaining a cow had not been easy. The closest animal of which they had any knowledge was the horse, reports of which had reached them from the very distant west – where Mexican refugees fleeing the destruction of their city had brought word of four-legged beasts that bore men upon their backs – but they had never laid eyes on one. Once I had established 'something in the manner of a horse' I mimed horns and udders, to the protests of my companions. 'This animal is called the cow,' I had said. 'From its head I take my name. Alvar Nuñez Cabeza de Vaca, at your service.'

First one smile, then another.

'Cow's Head!' they had roared.

Now, it seemed, Estevanico was laughing at me as well. A former slave. An infidel. I addressed him sternly.

'Your attitude discredits you,' I said in a stiff voice. 'Lowly as your station is, I have always respected you. You fought valiantly in La Florida, more so than some Christians, and bore the hardships of that march with fortitude and aplomb. You come from a noble lineage, the Moors who once ruled over Spain; your ancestors probably killed mine, and mine killed yours. It is not fashionable to admit, but sometimes, in those complex wars, they might have fought on the same side. Who can say? It is possible. In any case, we share a bond of history and of blood. I think it a shame that a man like you, a descendent of the armies of the caliphs of al-Andalus, should display the same vulgar humour as a bunch of heathens. It grieves me. It does not become you. I expected better.'

Having said my piece, I removed my hands from their saline bath and took a stubby iron nail from the pocket of my breeches. It was a memento from the raft, forged from melted spurs. I used it to push the dirt from under my fingernails.

Estevanico was silent for a time; I sensed that he was moved. When at last he spoke, his face was long and mournful.

'What can I say?' he said. 'Your name has always made me smile. Where I come from, the idea of adopting one's title from an animal is strange, even ridiculous. But who am I to judge? I do not even have a name. My parents called me Mustafa, which means Chosen One, but that name was taken from me when I became a slave. My master called me Estevan, after the Christian saint who was stoned to death by Jews, and then – because he was fond of me – he called me Estevanico. It means Little Estevan. It makes a child out of me. So I am known by a diminutive of a Christian name that is not even mine. What right do I have to find your name amusing?'

I considered this information for a while, delving with the nail. 'Do you wish me to call you Mustafa?' I asked.

He sighed and shook his head.

It was my turn to be silent then. Something tugged inside me that I did not understand. I suddenly felt that I might weep. In order to distract myself I jabbed the nail too deep and felt a stab of pain. I flung it to one side.

'It is not right, it is not right,' I said, 'to laugh at a person's name. The title Cabeza de Vaca has a long and noble past. It was bestowed on Martin Alhaja, my maternal ancestor, for his clever actions at the Cliff of Plunging Dogs. Alfonso VIII, King of Castile, was lost in the mountains with his knights…' I took a breath and found myself unable to continue with the story. I was savagely upset.

'What does it matter?' asked the Moor. 'The Indians who laughed at you are heathens and idolators. They worship fish and rocks and rain. The men wear rings through their penises. Allah only knows what the women do. Why should you care what they think of your name? Their own names sound like the squawks of mating monkeys.'

I could not explain to him. I rose from the fire and walked away, leaving him with the slumbering forms of Carranza and Maldonado, which, wrapped up in their blankets, more resembled corpses. My bare feet squelched in sucking sand as I wandered down the beach, wiping insects off my face, my heart strangely trembling. I walked until I could not see the light of the fire or the camp, until I reached the torrid swamp. Crabs scuttled in the dark. There were plops and croaks and whistles. I waded out a little way and waited there, up to my knees, for something to occur to me. I felt naked, empty.

'I have been stripped of everything,' I heard my voice say, small and weak. Tears dribbled down my cheeks. 'My dreams of gold. My dignity. My strength. The mercy of the Lord. It has all been taken from me. My name is all I have.'

They heard the howling back at camp, I was informed the following day. My cries of rage and my weird sobs echoed down the coastline. The noises poured out of me with violence I could not control. Carranza and Maldonado thought it the work of demons.

As I walked back up the beach – minutes or hours later, I had lost all sense of time – there was nothing left of me. I was something new.

The ceremony was performed with a cactus thorn, the nib of which was dipped in ink made from crushed-up sea-worms. At first two Karankawa men held me down, pressing my back upon the sand, but when they saw I did not struggle they relaxed their grip. A third man – some manner of priest – straddled me with his strong legs and worked away with the implement, jabbing it into my skin. The pain was constant and acute. It felt as if thousands of bees were stinging me in one place all at the same time. I would like to say that I bore the ordeal manfully, but I did not. I whimpered like a child.

When it was over they pulled me to my feet, my chest a sheet of blood. There were shouted accolades. Women slapped me on the back.

Carranza and Maldonado, who had obstinately refused to watch, now stared in disbelief. 'Mother of God,' said Carranza, 'what have you done to yourself?'

Maldonado quietly crossed himself and did not speak a word.

From my nipples to my neck my pale skin had been tattooed with a pattern of dark stripes. Looking down at the livid flesh, I did not recognise myself.

I washed the blood off in the sea, practically drunk with pain. It swirled in a muddy red cloud about my body.

My family coat-of-arms consists of an escutcheon chequy of gules and or on an azure field, or – for those unversed in heraldic terminology – a checkered shield of red and gold on a background of blue. Red and gold, of course, are the royal colours of Spain, the colours of blood and treasure, and perhaps the blue represents the sea that hems our country on three sides, the confines of which – thanks to the actions of a certain Genoan navigator in 1492 – we have now triumphantly torn ourselves free from.

Surrounding the shield are six cows' heads in the attitude of affronté. This means they are not displayed sinister or dexter – left or right – but face-on, staring fixedly in the direction of the viewer. There is challenge in their gaze. They are stern and strong. They are horned, blue-grey, with tufts of hair. I do not know why there are six of them; I suppose it is symmetry.

Ever since I was a boy I have felt an affinity with cows. I have admired their muscular grace, their sad eyes and their patience. From my travels in the New World I have learned that certain Indians have similar affinities with designated animals, believing them to be protectors or guides through the spirit realm. Their guardian angels take the forms of snakes and birds and lizards. I can relate to this belief, blasphemous as it might be; in the heat of battle I have sometimes felt my body to be surrounded by a protective halo not of divine light, but of six cows' heads.

My compatriots are better known for their fixation with bulls, against which hot-blooded young men, when they are not at war, pit themselves in wild displays of arrogance and acrobatics. I have never had an inclination for this savage pastime. Perhaps the source of my distaste has less to do with sympathy for the actual animal than it does with something else: the fact that, whenever I witness it, it is the symbol of my family that I see humiliated, goaded with painful darts and confused by colours and noise, its bravery rewarded with death before a jeering crowd. My father, may God rest his soul, did not seem at all perturbed by this – in fact my entire family gladly cheered the butchery – but I could never seem to divorce the bloody spectacle from the faces of the cows gazing from our coat-of-arms. To celebrate their belittlement was a kind of sacrilege.

Gules and or, with six cows' heads. This crest has accompanied me on every campaign I have fought, from Italy to La Florida. I have worn it on my shield and on my quilted tunic. But my shield was split at Apalachee, splintered by a volley of arrows as I crouched in jungle mud, and my tunic fell apart on our second week at sea. I used its rags to wipe the sweat from the face of a man who was dying of thirst, and then I tossed them over-board along some nameless coastline.

🐾

Carranza and Maldonado avoided my company for some time after the ordeal with the inky thorn. You might think this difficult in light of our close proximity, but under the circumstances it was not; I was mostly in a fever. My wounds had become infected, like meat spoiling in the sun, and I fell into a delirium that lasted for several weeks. Drifting in and out of sense and babbling incoherently, my chest an Islamic carpet of red, yellow, white and black, I was carried up the beach by a group of Karankawa women. When shadows washed over me it occurred to me that I was dying, and being prematurely buried, but in fact I was being laid in a house of convalescence. This was one of the dome-shaped dwellings, thatched with reeds from the swamp, that neither myself nor my companions had previously been allowed entrance to. From the outside we had thought them primitive and poorly made, but the interior was cool and comfortable. Through the waves of my delirium I watched dim figures come and go. Sunbeams fell through the slatted walls, and some manner of fine net, woven from I know not what, was draped across the entrance-way to keep the crawling flies away. It was the first time in months that I had experienced shade.

The fever was a slow fire smouldering beneath my skin, cooking me inside myself. My wounds reeked like a cheese. Estevanico, who was often at my side to apply the medicines that the Karankawa had prescribed – some ingested, some imbibed, some absorbed and some inhaled – kept patient vigil over me through the long, humid nights, exhausted as he must have been from his daily labours. He listened to the nonsense talk that poured unbidden from my lips; later I learned that I had babbled endlessly about shellfish – 'push, twist, push, twist' repeated like a liturgy – and had sobbed as I begged forgiveness from our poor murdered steeds, lying with their throats cut in the Bay of Horses. I had also often talked of my ancestor Martin Alhaja, of the Cliff of Plunging Dogs and the cow's skull standing on its rock. Once, in my befuddlement, I had mistaken Estevanico for the long-dead caliph of the Moors, imagining him returned from the grave to take his revenge on my family. It had taken several Indians to pin my body to the bed as I thrashed and raged.

I remember little of that time but muddled, sordid images. Perhaps this is for the best, for I suffered dreadfully. When, at last, the fever abated and my senses returned to me – the wounds healed on my chest, though the ink would never fade – I staggered back into the light with Estevanico as my crutch. My legs could hardly support my weight, even though I had starved for weeks. The hot sand under my naked feet was almost unbearable. The sea was shining bright that day and the swampland pools were dazzling, as if the whole universe was exploding in golden light.

'Here is the gold I never found,' I said, clinging to the Moor. His dark skin was drenched with it, gleaming like a statue. 'We are children of the sun!' I cried.

'Be calm now,' he said.

We went together down the beach to the place where my fellow Spaniards were. They were taking a break from oysters and were working their way through a heap of razor clams that stood about four feet high. The long brownish narrow shells lay discarded on the sand. Maldonado gazed at me through suffering, red-rimmed eyes.

'So you are recovered,' he said. 'We prayed for you every day.'

Carranza deftly slipped his blade between the fused lips of a shell and opened them with a twist, neatly flicking out the meat. He popped the morsel in his mouth and chewed and swallowed joylessly. His blond moustache went up and down, lank and unhappy. 'Your sickness was a punishment,' he said without looking at me, 'for debasing the flesh that the Lord clothed you in. Your fever was a taste of Hell, to warn you of the evil road these Indians will lead you down. Those marks upon your chest are bad, but the mark on your soul is worse.'

In my purged and weakened state, these words deeply affected me. My tongue could offer no reply so I simply squatted next to him and took up a handful of clams. But my fingers did not have the strength to prise the brittle shells apart; they clattered from my hands and I could not pick them up again.

'We have all walked evil roads,' I said, and they did not disagree.

When I had regained my strength I returned to my former toil, but something in the nature of the work seemed to have changed. Somehow the task felt more bearable – or at least less unbearable – than it had been before, as if my suffering had given me access to previously unexploited reservoirs of endurance. It was simple, repetitive, meditative, like fingering beads on a rosary. My hands performed mechanically and my mind was free to wander.

I had much to think about. In the latter stages of my recovery I had developed a powerful interest in Karankawa medicine, which – doubtless in conjunction with Maldonado's daily prayers – I credited with saving my life. The salves and balms and poultices, the bandages made from moss, the smoke from bitter herbs that had been wafted about my head and blown through hollow straws into my nostrils and my mouth; these had proved more effective than techniques I had known in Spain, and I endeavoured to learn as much about them as I could. The women who had cared for me endured my questions patiently and humoured me as they might a child; little by little I drew from them the secrets of their healing art. I learned which leaves brought down a fever and which induced vomiting, which cactuses, when milked for sap, could numb the mind and conquer pain, which slimy seaweeds thinned the blood or sterilised an infection. The discovery that pleased me best was that the oil of alligators, which I had observed both women and men to smear thickly upon their bodies, was worn not for aesthetic appeal but for its repelling effect on insects, which could not abide the smell. Delighted with this useful knowledge I stripped myself almost naked and generously applied the grease, then marched down to my comrades.

'No bothersome fly has come near me for the last half hour,' I said. 'Look, they dare not approach.' It was true: my presence had punched a hole in the black cloud of buzzing mites that surrounded the Spaniards and Estevanico; the air cleared around me as I walked and filled back in behind.

'I would rather suffer flies than cover my body in that filth,' said Carranza in disgust. 'You are darker than the Moor.'

There was a meaty smack as Maldonado swatted his neck, drawing back his palm to reveal a mess of splattered insect parts. He gazed at me beseechingly.

'Estevanico?' I offered.

Looking Carranza in the eye, the Moor scooped grease from off my arm and slathered it on like warpaint.

Within the hour Estevanico was as thickly oiled as me, and by the end of the afternoon Maldonado had succumbed. Carranza stoically endured the torment for another week, adopting an air of defiant contempt like a martyr being tortured for his faith, but there came the day – after swarms of flying ants turned the beach, and the surface of the sea, black with their multitudes – when he too appeared with gleaming oil-slick skin, eyes swivelling furiously as if daring a reaction. None of us said anything. The insects stayed away from us. This was the beginning of the general humbling.

My knowledge of the Karankawa language was improving by the day. The Indians were much amused by the childish mistakes I made, confusing one word with another and speaking in nonsense sentences, and once an old man took offence at an erroneous thing I had said – I never gleaned exactly what – and pursued me with a twisted stick to the laughter of all who witnessed it. Despite such setbacks, I was able to develop my abilities until I could speak in a pidgin that was broadly understood. The xs, qs and ks that had seemed so harsh at first came to lose their jagged edge, for I had heard them spoken gently, even tenderly, as I was lying in my state of convalescence. In a similar way most Indians, I have learned since then, initially find Castilian – so sweet and graceful to our ears – ugly and frightening due to the circumstances in which they first encounter it: invariably, I am sorry to say, as screamed commands on a battlefield or orders yelled at slavering hounds. But once my ears had learned to associate the syllables with amity, my tongue quickly mastered them and my fluency increased.

The grammar was somewhat more challenging, as it included tenses and even genders that were wholly unfamiliar to me. The Indians had no conception of linear time, as we do, but rather a series of wheels that infinitely repeated themselves; anchoring a particular action in the 'past', 'present' or 'future' required leaps of intuition that largely eluded me. Likewise they had no possessive nouns corresponding to 'mine' or 'yours', but only a general 'ours' that appeared to encompass everything, so that I found it impossible to understand relationships between one thing and another in any traditional sense. Most confusingly of all there were at least six separate genders – male, female, neuter, and three that remained beyond my ability to translate or comprehend – which were not fixed to particular objects but depended on that object's relationship with the other objects that it happened to be interacting with. A person, a vulture or a lump of rock might be male one day and female or something else the next. It was thoroughly perplexing.

I seldom spoke of these linguistic conundrums with Carranza or Maldonado, who took little interest in them, but sometimes confided in Estevanico when we were alone. He was the only one of us who had knowledge of other languages, Arabic being his primary tongue, although he had not used it in years for anything other than prayer.

'It is the language of God,' he said. 'But I have lost so much of it. It was taken from me with my name. Now I can only think and dream in the language my masters gave to me.'

'Perhaps the same will happen with me,' I said.

He looked at me strangely.

A fire was lit upon the beach and fistfuls of shellfish were hurled upon it by a laughing, singing crowd. The meat spat in the flames in a series of small explosions. It angered the Spaniards and Estevanico to see the fruits of our backbreaking labours wasted so wantonly, but to the Karankawa it was an appropriate offering, which their gods would reciprocate in the following year's harvest. 'The Israelites did much the same,' I reminded my companions. 'And do not Muslims sacrifice certain animals for their feasts? In fact, was not the Lamb of God sacrificed for all mankind? His fire was the cross and we are all His harvest…' They did not reply; the clamour around us was too great. All four of us were stripped to the waist and our torsos smeared with paint, a condition of celebration that our hosts had insisted upon, and additionally our beards – now of a length and volume that greatly impressed the Indians, to whom the Lord, mysteriously, had not allotted facial hair apart from the scantiest wisps – were waxed with alligator grease and sculpted into outlandish shapes. We wore flowers in our hair and garlanded around our necks. We had also partaken of a beverage made from fermented grains, which, on the third or fourth taste, was not completely unpalatable. This being the first alcoholic drink that had passed our lips in a year, all of us were in a state of advanced intoxication.

'What is it that drives them to this act?' I heard Maldonado cry. He was squatting by the fire. I presumed that his words referred to some heathen revelry – the painted bodies jostling together or the dancers in shaggy masks who leapt and whirled among the crowd – but his eyes were fixed instead on the countless tiny beetles which, drawn by the light of the fire, were determinedly marching to their deaths. The more I looked the more I saw: legions, armies, nations of them. It was a doomed crusade. The embers of the fire were haloed with charred corpses.

'That was us in La Florida,' said Carranza in a slurred voice. His movements were unsteady as he stooped towards the sand. 'Look, there goes our great leader Narvaez…' He plucked up one of the beetles between his finger and his thumb, examined it lazily and then tossed it on the pyre.

'May he rest in peace,' said Maldonado as the beetle popped and writhed. The faces of both men were monstrous in the shadows and orange light.

The moon was full in the sky, glaucous and malevolent, bulging through an ethereal mist that was wafting at an unreal speed through the universe. A memory came to me of a full moon over Cadiz on the night we had sailed from Spain; masts creaking in the port and the smell of bitter oranges. Would I see such a sight again? And if I did, might it be the case that the eyes I saw it through might have changed so drastically that it would not be the same?

I became aware of a chant that was building on the beach, keeping in time with the pounding drums.

'Cow's Head!' they were shouting. 'Cow's Head! Cow's Head! Cow's Head!'

The crowd parted as I walked. Children grinned and giggled. The priest was waiting by the sea, decked out in his finery. I could not see the implement but it was long and slender.

This time I did not require two Indians to hold me down. My feet were planted solidly. I bit my lip but did not scream as he pushed it through my nipple.

First through the left, then through the right. Blood dribbled in black streams. Then through the septum of my nose and through my bottom lip and finally through my earlobes, which were almost like an afterthought. The pain was commensurate; no more than what it was.

Plugs of sharks' teeth and carved bone now graced me at my punctured points. As I walked back up the beach many Indians walked behind me.

I felt happy, as if I had joined a feast in some great echoing hall.

I danced. My three companions danced. We moved our limbs rhythmically, our eyelids squeezed tightly shut, pulled – as our raft had been – into a rising current that would not let us go.

At last that season came to an end. The oysters were diminished. The fresh piles grew lower and lower, like a depleting mountain range, until we were merely crouching in the foothills of eviscerated shells and staring at the beach's level plain as it stretched away. There were footsteps on that beach. The Karankawa were leaving. Around us the dwellings were being dismantled into their component parts, the sticks and reeds returned to the swamp from which they had been cut. The idols of the heathen gods – eyeless, crude and sexless things that at first had horrified us but which now we hardly saw – were removed from their wooden plinths; some were burned, some buried. Some of the tribe left in boats, threading a path through the labyrinthine channels and sandbars of the coast according to obscure maps made of knotted twine, but most of them simply walked.

The four of us walked with them.

Shellfish season, eel season, fowl season, flounder season, the season of cactus fruits and the season of edible roots: those brackish wastes were bountiful for those with eyes to see. The Karankawa moved throughout the year from one location to the next, following cyclical patterns of scarcity and abundance, never exhausting one supply before moving on again. They seldom ventured far inland – firm ground did not much interest them – but made their home, or their various homes, in the parts where land and water met, the shifting intertidal realms between solid and liquid. They travelled in a similar manner to their conception of time, which was never in a straight line – as we had done on our simple course from the Old World to the New – but always looping back again to the places they had left. In this way they did not live one lifetime but a series of lifetimes, each one a permutation on the ones that had gone before. Cleaving to them as we were, we lived those lifetimes too.

Four years we travelled on that coast. One year for each of us.

We learned the use of bows and spears, to hunt and to fish and to trap. Occasionally we joined them in their brief, indecisive wars. Those skirmishes with neighbouring tribes were quite unlike our own campaigns, being less strategic than symbolic, and were not intended to end disputes but rather to sustain them. Indeed Carranza was reprimanded for his martial enthusiasm, for once his warrior blood was up there was no stopping him, and his reckless charges at the foe – accompanied by the Spanish cry of 'For God and Santiago!', which my ancestors would have known on the plains of Castile – were considered to have broken some obscure taboo. Nevertheless he proved his courage, which was enough for him, and his antics on the battlefield restored a little of the pride that had been so dented by the shame of circumstance. He lost his resentment and his scorn, although he was never able to look at my altered body without a scowl. Perhaps it was jealousy.

Maldonado and Estevanico found their places in other ways. Maldonado took an Indian wife and had a child by her, although the infant sadly died during a summer plague. He buried her in the Christian fashion and claimed her soul was now with God, the first – and, I suspect, the last – of the Karankawa to find their way to Heaven. He became a thoughtful man after that, quiet and philosophical, and spent his time whittling crucifixes to distribute to the Indians, who accepted them as gifts but showed minimal curiosity for what they represented. Estevanico, meanwhile, became adept at tracking and trapping the alligators from which we obtained the insect-repelling oil, and won much acclaim for this. He also became a skilled navigator, which would serve the four of us well in the years to come.

As for myself, I studied the art of medicine as best I could. By combining Indian knowledge with the techniques I had known in Spain – hot cupping, the letting of blood, a basic grasp of humour theory and rudimentary surgery learned on the battlefields of my career – I became known along that coastline as a healer. Rumours spread among neighbouring tribes of a pale, hair-covered medicine man who did not charge for his services but only asked for snippets of knowledge: fragments of other languages, the locations of neighbouring territories, news about wars and alliances, heathen spiritual beliefs. In that way, my mental horizons gradually expanded. Inland from that hurricane-wracked coast there stretched a vast continent – I heard stories of plains, branching rivers, deserts, mountain ranges, great forests, people who lived in deer-hide tents and people who lived in cities of stone – and, as my proficiency in Indian languages increased, it no longer seemed inconceivable that I might find some way through it.

'I think it is time to leave,' I said one night to my companions as we sat beside our fire. We were sharing a cup of Indian wine, which was made of cactus sap and gave a pleasurable burn.

'Where?' Estevanico asked.

'To Mexico,' I said.

'To find gold?'

'To find home.'

'How?'

'I will walk.'

Carranza pulled at his blond moustache and stared intensely at the fire. Little dancing yellow flames were reflected in his eyes. Maldonado looked down at the face of his sleeping wife, whose head was resting on his knee, and blinked his eyelids heavily as if he was about to cry.

Estevanico took my hand. 'How will you find your way?' he asked.

'I will follow the sun,' I said.

𝔁

When I asked the Karankawa if we could be given our freedom they did not appear to understand the question. 'Your spirits have gone already,' they said. 'So you must catch up with them.'

On the night before we left, I told the tribe a story.

𝔁

Alfonso VIII, King of Castile, was lost in the mountains with his knights. This was in Andalucia, which takes its name from al-Andalus, the name given it by the Moors who ruled Spain in those days. They were Muslims from Africa, infidels who did not know Christ, and they had built great fortresses and domed mosques with tiled walls and windmills and water-mills and planted groves of citrus trees. For five hundred years the Christian kings had pushed their borders slowly south, reconquering one square inch of bloodsoaked earth at a time, and now Alfonso rode at the head of an army drawn from every part of Spain to fight the Moorish caliph who was waiting on the plain.

The infidel army was better positioned, better provisioned and better armed; the caliph himself was protected by a bodyguard of chained slaves.

61

Alfonso's knights had been lost for days, dismayed by the deep ravines and the precipitous snowbound peaks, unable to find their way through the mountains. The king was on the point of giving up. Then a saviour came.

He was not a noble knight or an angel with a burning sword, but a simple shepherd, roughly shod, with a wineskin hanging at his side. He told the king of a secret pass that no one knew about but him, and promised that he would mark its entrance with a sign. The next day Alfonso's army made its way between the walls of rock to emerge behind the Moorish camp, taking their enemies by surprise. They won a famous victory there, routing the Muslims from the plain; the caliph fled with his life but left his tent and standard behind, which was a great dishonour for him. In their panic to escape, many of his soldiers fell to their deaths from the top of a ravine. Ever since then it has been known as the Cliff of Plunging Dogs, as the place where we killed our steeds is known as the Bay of Horses.

After that battle, which was a turning point in the centuries-old reconquest of Spain, King Alfonso rewarded the shepherd with a title and a coat of arms. The shepherd's name had been Martin Alhaja but now he was known as Cabeza de Vaca, after the secret sign with which he had marked the pass: a cow's skull on a rock, sun-bleached, with empty eyes.

That shepherd – now a nobleman – was my maternal ancestor.

That was how my family got the name Cow's Head.

Now the force of that reconquest has spilled across the sea, a wave that has built for hundreds of years, bearing its inheritors from al-Andalus to this New World. We carry the symbols we have won, though their meanings might have changed. We have passed through the narrow passageway and emerged into the light.

And so we begin to walk, three Spaniards and a Moor washed up on the edge of this continent. We trace a wide brown river inland and leave the coast behind. Ahead of us rises a shadowed line that might be clouds or hills or smoke. Each of us wears an oyster shell around our necks like pilgrims.

'Past', 'present' and 'future' do not serve; the Karankawa are right. From my journey I have learned that time does not flow in a straight line but turns inside repeating wheels, so that everything that has happened is still happening. Nothing has ever stopped. It will never stop. We are still limping west, following the turning sun which spills its gold on our backs at dawn and on our faces at dusk. We are crossing mountains, salt plains, deserts of cracked rock. We are passing through countries that no European and no African has seen before, and recording the names of nations never before chronicled: Camone, Charruco, Han, Quitole, Como, Cuayo, Atayo, Cuchendado. We are walking in the shadow of change, for sickness is spreading through the land and cities are emptying, gods are dying, ash is drifting everywhere. People have started following us, the lost following the lost: runaways and refugees, the downcast and the dispossessed, people who have fallen through history like the caliph's soldiers fell – are falling still, on time's great wheel – and have not yet hit the earth. I call them Children of the Sun. I heal them, guide them, preach to them, across this changing continent. They are all Cow's Heads, half one thing and half another.

It takes eight years to reach Mexico. Two years for each of us.

We arrive in the province of New Spain. The last of our followers drifts away. Our countrymen stare at our bleeding feet and our ropes of matted hair.

The city has been renamed. The heathen temples have been pulled down and cathedrals erected in their place. Down cobbled lanes walk lines of slaves. The lake is being drained.

'What is your name?' demands the official at his paper-covered desk.

I open my mouth but nothing comes. A fly bumps off the walls.

Green Bang

❦

$54 trillion a year
Estimated upper value of the world's
natural capital and ecosystem services

It was a warm autumn day, and the ecosystem service providers were buzzing in the natural capital. The foliage was consuming the light. Anders was sitting in his usual chair. Sophie and Sasha were on their way, and this afternoon he would go with Sasha to an area of outstanding natural beauty to forge a closer familial connection while recreationally walking.

No, that was not correct. Anders rubbed his head with his thumb. It wasn't an area of outstanding natural beauty, it was twelve hectares or thereabouts of medium to low quality indigenous fauna habitat, but Sasha need not be concerned about that. Sasha was nine years old. The place was pretty – yes, it was pretty – its cultural and recreational value was adequate for their purposes, and such qualitative definitions, he thought, were not of importance to children.

Such definitions were not of importance. Anders closed and re-opened his eyes. He gazed at his trouser legs stretched across the patio, and then at the pebbles around the lawn and the trees beyond the garden. The trees were mostly rowans and oaks, and during a night of sleeplessness that had occurred some months ago he had calculated the value of each to about 600 ecos a year – taking into account such factors as sequestration of atmospheric carbon, electricity conservation through shading and wind reduction, interception of particulate matter, and raising property values through leaf surface area. He looked at them now, doing their part. It was a ballpark estimate, and something about it bothered him now. The leaves were moving in the light. He rose from his usual chair and took a few paces, frowning.

He had woken up with that ache again, the one behind his collarbones. Every morning for the past few weeks – a dull, familiar bruising. He took a few paces and stopped, absently rubbing around his neck, and then checked his phone to see the time. They would be here any minute. He turned to go back into the house, wondering if he should change his jumper. He thought the last time had gone quite well. Sophie had cooked them all a meal, and then he had taken Sasha to the multiplex to watch a film. The film had been a good idea, because it had given them shared points of reference. Even if they hadn't discussed it – her mother had wanted her home straight after – Anders hoped the experience might connect them still.

The film had been about cartoon animals fleeing the effects of a supervolcano, but his recollection of the plot was vague. Some had escaped and some had perished, but he couldn't remember how, or why, or what situation the animals had been in when the film ended. He thought back to Sasha's face, impassive in the light of the screen, the way he had strained to look at her without her knowing he was looking. He hadn't really been able to tell whether or not she'd enjoyed it.

He found himself at the end of the garden, and suddenly realised he was crying. Well, perhaps he wasn't *crying* – but water was coming from his eyes, and he didn't know how he had got there. He'd thought he was going into the house. He was going to change his jumper. Wiping with the backs of both hands, he realised he didn't feel sad, could think of nothing to be sad about. Confused, he retraced his steps, and by the time he had reached the back door the phenomenon had ceased. He looked back towards the trees, the rowans and oaks holding and increasing their value year by year, converting energy from the sun into fungible units of worth, diligently running through their economic functions.

Ironically, it was an economy he was no longer useful to, practically no longer part of. After all he'd done, he was finished now, relegated to the role of consumer – and these days, hardly even that. His consumption levels were negligible. When she had first visited here, a sort of preparatory check ahead of Sasha's visit today, Sophie had accused him of being a hermit. Actually it felt as if every word she spoke to him, since she'd started speaking to him again, was an accusation of some kind, and he'd long since abdicated the right to defend himself. He was in the house now, moving through his possessions. Evidence of former worldly engagement was displayed haphazardly: dusty flatscreen monitors from the days when he still traded from home, a few framed photographs dating back to the early Bang, technology he no longer noticed but most of which was worth many times the value of the trees outside. His jumper was draped on the back of a chair. He pulled it over his head and walked through the room putting it on, bumping into furniture. They would be here any minute. He checked his phone again.

There wasn't much to do inside, so he returned to the garden. There was something about those trees, something he hadn't got right. It bothered him and he didn't know why. His collarbones still ached. He went to where the trees began and laid his hand on the nearest trunk, feeling the coolness of the bark and thinking automatically of the process of evapotranspiration cooling the air around his home, the calculations that flowed from that – suddenly he felt tired. He pressed his forehead to the trunk. An ecosystem service provider was fumbling a path through the branches, colliding with the lower leaves, heading to its next pollination event. He watched it stagger drunkenly, and felt a small surge of affection. As a younger man he had made, and lost, a large amount of money on pollinators, buying forest habitat credits on behalf of tropical coffee plantations – until commodity prices had plunged, the coffee was replaced by pineapple groves to which pollination services were an active hindrance, the forest ceased to serve any purpose and the credits had depreciated in value by tens of thousands of ecos. But he was young then, starting out – he'd bounced back from things like that. Was it affection he felt, or nostalgia? Sometimes he missed who he had been. The service provider went on its way. The day was warm but wet weather was coming. Soon it would be redundant.

He realised he had become distracted, and retreated to the middle of the lawn in order to look at the trees as a whole. Six hundred ecos a year, a rough calculation. But the oaks were surely worth more than the rowans, both in terms of services rendered, due to their greater size, and their leaf surface area appeal – maybe even *cultural* appeal. How to quantify that? He took a few paces back. One and a half rowans, say, might equate to a single oak – was that a possible starting point? The canopies were starting to brown. A couple of leaves detached themselves from the branch he was looking at and made their slow way down to earth, and that was when it jolted him: never mind the conversion rate between trees, what was the value of a *leaf*? He felt a tingling of nerves. The sensation was familiar but it made him nervous. Hurriedly, to get the thing over with quickly, he selected a sample branch and estimated its number of leaves, multiplied that by the number of branches – an even wilder estimate that gave him 180,000 – then divided 600 into that. It gave him 0.0033 ecos, or 0.33 cents, per leaf. Approximately three leaves to the cent. Three hundred leaves to the eco. He felt slightly sick in the warmth of the day. He might have to take off his jumper. Stooping around the lawn he began to sort them into piles, each pile representing one unit, counting under his breath as he went: 57, 58, 59… 125, 126, 127… 297, 298, 299, *one unit* of natural capital… then he straightened up, feeling ridiculous. He knew he should turn around.

'Dad.' She was in the garden, wearing wellies and a purple coat. Sophie was watching from the door, and Anders had the immediate impression that Sasha had been silently coaxed to utter the first word of greeting – he imagined a series of urgent mimes taking place between them, Sophie encouraging, Sasha refusing, until her mother's will won out. Now she had accomplished her task the girl was staring at her feet.

'What are you doing?' Sophie asked.

'Tidying leaves,' he said. There was a moment of silence, during which he dropped some leaves. 'How did you get here?'

'We drove,' Sophie said.

'No, in the garden.'

'The front door was open.'

'Hello, Sasha,' he said to his daughter. He bent at the knee and hugged her awkwardly, conscious of Sophie's critical eye.

'Hi,' said Sasha again. She created a small smile.

Sophie came out, but there was no hug. She touched him on the arm. 'Shall we go inside?' she said. 'I've got sandwich stuff.'

'I bought her a present.'

'Tell her, not me.'

'I bought you a present.'

'Thank you,' said Sasha. But once they were inside the house he forgot where it was – even *what* it was. He was feeling unpleasantly warm again, but didn't want to remove his jumper for fear his shirt might smell of sweat. Sophie had gone into the kitchen and was slicing bread for sandwiches.

Her familiarity with his home seemed less personal than professional, like a social service provider doing a house call.

Sasha sat on the edge of the sofa, her wellies dangling over the floor. Anders liked seeing her there, but he didn't know what to say.

'How are you?' he asked, hovering near.

'I'm okay.'

'How's school?'

'It's okay. I like Mrs MacGregor.' She thought for a while. 'I don't like games.'

'We're going for a walk.'

'I know.'

'Are you driving?' asked Sophie, bringing the sandwiches. She was facing him but he knew that her eyes were peripherally focused on the room, evaluating his living conditions. He wished he'd remembered to clean up.

'No, it's just along the road. An area of low quality indigenous… outstanding… natural habitat.' The words were getting mixed up before they reached his mouth. Sophie was looking at him oddly. 'A *woodland, woods*,' he managed to say, but it came out strangled.

'Are you alright?' she asked at the door, when Sasha had gone on ahead. 'You seem a bit distracted. Or something. If this isn't a good time…'

'It is a good time.'

'We can do this another weekend.'

'It's good. I'm looking forward to it.'

'Try to relax. She's just a bit shy. She wants to like you, you know.'

They felt like the nicest words she had said to him for a long time, but immediately he wasn't sure. What did that mean, exactly? Anyway, there were no more concessions, and when they parted at the car her eyes were alert and distant. She kissed the top of Sasha's head, told her she'd be back at three, nodded to Anders in a manner that seemed exaggeratedly formal, and a moment later the car was gone and father and daughter were standing alone.

'Right,' said Anders, pointlessly. A helicopter flew overhead. Brown leaves descended from the trees, economic units that had served their usefulness.

They walked together side by side, Anders holding the carrier bag, Sasha scuffing in her boots which were a little oversized, past the golf course, the ice hockey centre and a pre-developed development site, until they reached the start of the trees. 'Protected Natural Habitat Area' was displayed on the entrance sign, and a system of green stars indicated its biological, cultural/recreational and sequestration values, none of them especially high – in fact, Anders thought they were lower than when he had last come here. Two square posts indicated the starting points of the Common Toad and Hedgehog Trails, each with its cartoon representation of the indigenous creature in question, along with statistics about the services each provided. The common toad wore sunglasses, and the hedgehog had a little hat. Woodchip pathways sliced through the trees in two different directions.

'Which way shall we go?' asked Anders.

Sasha shrugged.

'Which one do you like the look of most?'

She pointed to the one in the hat. 'Are there hedgehogs?' she asked with hope.

'Theoretically there could be,' he said as they set off down the path. 'That is, it's a suitable habitat. But I don't know much about their habits or current distribution. We might not actually see them.' Sasha didn't respond to this. He wished he was better at talking to children. The path was wide enough to walk abreast but she seemed to want to walk slightly behind him, and they progressed like this for a couple of minutes without saying anything more. He analysed the quietness, and didn't think it felt so bad – it was better to walk in silence, at least, than sit in silence in a room. The ache beneath his collarbones seemed to have subsided.

They wouldn't see hedgehogs here, he knew. There weren't enough green stars. These woods were less than ten years old – some of the smaller trees still wore protective mesh cylinders, though what protected the trunks against he couldn't quite imagine. These twelve hectares of medium to low quality habitat had been forested by a soft drinks company, offset against a single hectare of rare/endangered species habitat somewhere in Spain, he seemed to recall, which the company needed to develop – he couldn't remember the species involved, but he thought it was some kind of snail. He knew this because he'd taken an interest when the deal went through. He'd long been out of the game by then, but the existence value of a natural habitat area near his home had been higher than he'd anticipated

– although of course there was no telling how long its existence might actually last. Like everything else in the world, it was only waiting its turn.

One hectare for twelve, he thought to himself. It seemed scarcely credible now. He couldn't even begin to guess what the rate might be in today's climate, the markets booming and crashing with increasing randomness, positive feedback mechanisms kicking in all over the place. He couldn't keep up with it any more. It wasn't like in the early days, when things had at least been *predictably* unstable. It was a different market now. It no longer made any sense.

The woods were quiet, apart from the sound of traffic rushing down the nearest road. Service providers of various kinds were active in the undergrowth, and intermittent birdsong added bioacoustic appeal. He realised he had dimly imagined the little girl would be somehow running, jumping over water features, chasing fritillaries. He felt very anxious all of a sudden. He listened to her dutiful footsteps on the path behind, the rustle of her jacket as she moved her arms. What was she *thinking*?

'Do you like it here?' he asked.

'It's pretty,' she said.

Anders felt a wave of relief quite out of proportion to her words – he felt almost dizzy with it. 'It is,' he said. 'I'm so glad we agree. Pretty places are important. They have high aesthetic and recreational value, some might even say spiritual value. The world would be a worse place without them.'

There was silence again after that. He wished she would start a conversation for once, so it wasn't always down to him. But that was ridiculous, she was only nine years old. He tried to picture himself through her eyes: an awkward stranger who was attempting, for reasons she probably didn't understand, to fit himself inside her life where he hadn't fitted before. Uncomfortably dressed, unapproachably tall, seemingly incomprehensible. She wanted to like him, Sophie had said. And he wanted her to like him too. If both of them wanted the same thing, then surely it couldn't be so hard. What had Sophie said about him? Did she know the mistakes he'd made?

He was pretty sure she knew nothing about him – about who he was, or who he had been. How could she be expected to know? Her rubber boots scrunched on the path. There was a pigeon somewhere. The trees were more spindly round here, the foliage less mature. How many visits, he wondered, to a medium to low quality habitat might equate to a single visit to a pristine boreal forest? Was there a qualitative rate of exchange – the way that, in a bygone age, two pilgrimages to certain shrines had been worth one to Rome? It was the kind of thing he'd once have discussed in the bar after work, a half-forgotten lifetime ago.

Twenty years ago, even ten. He found it almost impossible reaching his mind back to those times. His daughter might see him as shabby and odd, but he'd been part of something great. Someday, when she was older, he'd explain it all to her – how his generation had opened the world, how they'd changed *everything*.

Seized with sudden urgency, he opened his mouth to tell her this – but could find no starting point. He cleared his throat instead, squeezed shut his eyes. The problem was, his head got so full – he had to make a conscious effort to simplify the complexity. He found that his breath was short. The ache had returned.

Presently they came to a stream, not much more than two foot wide, with a sign that detailed its provisioning, regulating and recreational services scored by the usual green stars, which he didn't look at. The water was spanned by a little bridge, and as they stepped onto the bridge Anders, in a kind of desperate inspiration, reached down and took his daughter's hand. He amazed himself with this action – he had done it without thinking. Sasha's fingers stiffened in shock. She didn't pull away, at least. He realised his heart was beating fast, pounding beneath his shirt – this is ridiculous, he thought. But he felt very pleased.

'It's nice to see you,' he said. 'It's nice to go for a walk with you. I know you don't always… understand me. I mean, I try to make myself clear. But you'll get to know me, and I'll get to know you. Our relationship will improve.'

Silence. Of course there was silence – what possible answer could she give? Her shyness and embarrassment were like a cloud keeping pace with her, as his own kept pace with him, moving at the speed of travel. But she didn't pull away. They walked on for a minute like this as the trail looped through the planted woods, and, not wanting to say any more, he silently counted the steps they took. It averaged at one and a half of hers to every one of his.

They ate their designated picnic in the designated picnic area, where wooden tables and benches were set alongside recycling bins shaped like hedgehogs and common toads. They were near the edge of the woods again, within proximity of the road, but the trees were rustling with wind power so the traffic was less audible than it had been before. Anders sat on one side of the table, and Sasha on the other. The picnic was comprised of cheese and pickle sandwiches, trail mix, chocolate bars, banana yoghurts and carton drinks. Anders wasn't remotely hungry, but Sasha consumed her share with quiet diligence. He offered her his chocolate bar, but she shook her head and averted her eyes in a manner that seemed almost chaste.

'It's meant to be for you,' she said.

He put it in his top pocket.

Despite the fact he had held her hand, which made him glow when he thought of it, he still didn't know what to say to her, how to keep a conversation running beyond the initial sentences. He had had no practice at all. She looked so much like her mother, so little like him – although perhaps he didn't have the ability to judge. He hadn't known her for the greater proportion of her life. He had sent cards, of course, birthday and seasonally suitable presents, and he had paid the appropriate share towards her upbringing. But until very recently, when Sophie's force of will had impelled them back into contact, he had accepted the fact of his daughter's existence only in the abstract. Part of him had assumed he deserved this – part of him had been happy to escape. Now the gratitude he felt was rather startling.

It was already too late, he supposed, for his presence to ever be normal to her. She understood the world through his absence – this condition was fixed in her now, and probably could not be changed, no matter how many recreational walks they might engage in. Shifting baseline syndrome, that was what they called it once. What you consider normal as a child is what you consider normal as an adult, whether your background habitat is severely degraded or anything else. Certainly his own baseline had shifted more than once in his lifetime – for two decades he'd managed to keep pace with it, the peak and plateau of his career, before that grand systemic wobble that had ended everything. He could hardly claim to be keeping up now, keeping up with any of it – a hermit, Sophie had said. Was that a joke? He supposed it was funny. But the system had grown too complicated. His course over the last few years was less a retreat than a simplification.

He watched his daughter as she ate, secretly, as if looking for clues. She was a self-contained unit, an existence entirely separate from his. She was wearing a purple coat. She had banana yoghurt at the corner of her mouth. The merest fact of her sitting there was astonishing to him. He felt a pulse of despair: surely he would never understand her life, as she would never understand his. Today he might be obsolete, a historical irrelevance in the Green Bang's fading afterglow – but, once upon a time, he had added value to the world. That was the worth of his life, no matter what her mother might say.

It was the last great liberalisation, deregulation's final frontier. He had started off in carbon credits, like most of his contemporaries, buying and selling the right to emit sanctioned units of pollution. It was hardly groundbreaking work, but the theoretical sleight of hand that such an industry involved – transforming a negative externality into a buyable, sellable asset – had put him in a good position to expand into the other derivative markets taking shape at the time: pollination service provision, biodiversity offsetting, riparian and wetland banking, endangered species credits. He had been in the right place at the right time. All he had done, along with perhaps a thousand other bright young things in no more than half a dozen fortuitously placed companies, was to take the next logical step. The dominant global trend was comprehensive deregulation – the climate was highly favourable. He made great money. He travelled a lot. It was around this time he'd met Sophie. There was a sense that the world was changing, that he was a part of that change. How many people could say that, looking back on their lives? Once natural units were quantified, once they were fully fungible, it became possible to trade across different markets – to exchange endangered species credits, say, for carbon equivalent or peat bog futures, depending on the market rate. As more and more assets of natural capital were absorbed and integrated, there was exponential expansion. A critical mass was achieved: the green economy exploded. He and Sophie were living together. His office overlooked the Thames – itself transformed, in the new paradigm, from a greasy tidal river to a super-prime provisioning and regulating water service provider. He was one of the Men Who Sold the World, as the media termed it. He and Sophie argued a lot. The market grew to include streams and mountains, icecaps, wetlands and high chaparrals, every conceivable biotic unit from apex predators to bottom-feeders. Speculation had begun on complex systems such as ocean currents, forest biomes, mycelium networks, wholesale ecosystems – there was no upper limit. He was a high-net-worth individual. Of course there were warning signs. Did Sophie get pregnant around then? It was all a little disordered.

When things had gone wrong, they had gone wrong fast. Anders couldn't actually recall… he felt very tired all of a sudden. The day was warm, and leaves were falling. Sasha still had banana yoghurt at the corner of her mouth.

'Dad?' She was glancing down into her hand at what he realised was a mobile phone. 'Mum wants to know what time we'll be back.'

'Oh.' It was an effort to think. 'What… what time is it now?'

'It's twenty to three. She's coming at three.'

'Oh. Yes. We'll be home by then.' He watched as her thumbs tapped out a message. It made her look unexpectedly older. He noticed, for the first time, that she had earrings in her ears, and wondered if they had been there before. 'You have yoghurt…' She raised her head. 'Yoghurt, just beside your mouth.'

She wiped it away with a solemn expression, which made her look like a child again. She put the phone in her pocket. Anders put the rubbish in the bag. A yoghurt pot. A small plastic spoon. It felt too soon to leave.

'Sasha?'

'Yes?' Her solemnity grew, as if she sensed they were nearing that time – one of those adult conversations she'd probably learned to dread already. A siren whooped once, far away. She sat there very still.

'I want to tell you a story,' he said.

He took a deep, steadying breath.

'There was a time, before you were born, when a tree was just a tree… that's all it was, just that. And it was the same for other things. A mountain, a waterfall and a blade of grass were once just a mountain, a waterfall and a blade of grass. A bee was once just a bee. There was no reason for them.'

She gazed at him with worried eyes. He knotted his hands on the picnic table and concentrated on the words, on simplifying the complexity.

'And even longer before you were born, before even I was born – before there were bees, or dinosaurs, or single-celled organisms, or anything else you might have heard about – the world itself, the planet we live on, that had no reason either. It was only a ball of minerals waiting for something to happen to it, for something to give it meaning.'

'Then people came along, and for a long time we had no meaning either – we just happened to exist, like all the other things. But eventually we learned. We learned how to *value*. First we learned how to value ourselves, and then we learned how to value all the other things around us – the trees, the bees, the elephants, the rain, the ground beneath our feet. Suddenly everything had a value, had a meaning, that it never had before. Nothing exists for no reason now. There is meaning everywhere. Sasha, do you understand? Do you know what value is?'

It wasn't a question, and she didn't answer.

'It's another word for love. How can we love what has no value? The total love that's in the world is the total value of the world, all its units added up – its leaves, its blades of grass, its reserves and its carbon sinks, its systems and processes… like the maths you do in school. Everything added together.' Anders took another breath. His hands felt oddly far away, and something was happening to his eyes – a familiar throbbing. Sasha hadn't spoken, hadn't moved. Wind power was stirring the trees, rustling the natural capital. Everything would be alright. 'That is to say… what I mean…' The phenomenon was occurring again. Water was coming from his eyes, turning the world into rainbow prisms, yet once again he did not feel sad – instead, he felt elated. He wiped and snorted, and managed to say, 'I *value you* very much,' before covering up his face and breathing wetly into his hands. He stayed that way for a while.

When he had taken his hands away, Sasha was no longer at the table. But she hadn't gone far. Blearily he made her out, over by the recycling bins. He rose a little unsteadily and made his way to join her.

'Hey. It's alright,' he said.

'I know.'

'Everything will be fine.'

She shrugged unhappily. She looked even more like a child.

'What are you doing?'

'Clearing up. It's ten to three. Mum's coming at three.'

'Yes, we should be getting back.' He watched as she separated the rubbish and fed it through the appropriate mouths, paper and cardboard in the hedgehog, plastic in the common toad. The colours stood out bright and strong. The hedgehog looked very brown and the toad looked very green. Even after this natural habitat area had been exchanged, the fungible services it provided transposed to another sector of the world, Anders knew this was one of those moments that he would always remember.

Sophie's car was in the drive, and she was sitting by the door. She gave Anders a funny look but didn't say anything. They went inside and Anders made tea. They drank the tea in the living room. Sasha had a fizzy drink instead. Sophie asked Sasha if she'd enjoyed the walk, and she said that she had. The woods were pretty, she said again. They talked about this and that.

'I'll ring you soon,' Sophie said as they left. 'Please look after yourself.'

'Thanks for having me,' said Sasha. They hugged on the step.

Two minutes after they'd gone, Anders remembered the present he'd bought. But by the time he'd located it, in a bag hanging on the kitchen door, the car had vanished from the drive. It was a woolly hat and gloves decorated with polar bears, penguins and other nostalgic Arctic-themed animals, emblems of the icy past. It would have to wait until next time. Anyway, it was too warm.

He went upstairs and had a shower, then dressed again in the same set of clothes. There was mud on the trouser legs. He made his way back downstairs. He felt something against his chest and discovered the chocolate bar in his pocket, not melted yet, but on its way. He unwrapped it standing up, gazing around the familiar room. Dark, heavy furniture, expensive but a little worn. On the shelf, a squeezy rubber globe he'd once had on an office desk. He wandered to the garden again and took a seat in his usual chair. The rowans and oaks bordered the lawn. He slowly consumed the chocolate bar, watching the trees and the light.

He hadn't finished the story, of course. Sophie would probably do it for him, one of these days when Sasha was grown – when their relationship involved more than watching cartoon films and going on recreational walks. She would tell the other side, if Sasha didn't know it already. But at least he had attempted to give her the bigger picture.

It was all a little disordered. When things had gone wrong, they had gone wrong fast – or perhaps they'd been going wrong for a while. He'd already moved out by then. A temporary thing, as he recalled – they couldn't be in the same house. The baby was due in a couple of months, and he couldn't think of that. There was a downturn in floodplain banking that was concerning, but manageable. A few analysts were warning that rainforest credit ratings in certain sectors of the market were unrealistically high, that low quality assets had been parcelled up with higher ones, but these concerns were ignored. There had been warning signs, but he hadn't paid attention.

It was commonly said that no one saw it coming, but of course that wasn't true. Some people had seen it coming, as some people always did. Some people had made outrageous fortunes, as some people always did. A few canny hedge funds made a killing – humans are an infinitely adaptive species, after all. He just hadn't been one of them when positive feedback mechanisms turned millions of square miles of rainforest into tinder in an astoundingly short space of time, wiping billions of ecos off the market – sequestration, species, services, existence, the whole portfolio. The Amazon Basin Credit Crash, as it was later to be known, precipitated the other collapses: icecap reserves, coral reef futures, a whole raft of obscure derivatives like Sahel desertification mitigation credits, many of which he'd never even heard of – everything was interlinked. He hadn't moved fast enough. He had been wiped out.

Of course it wasn't the end of the world. A gold rush immediately began on remaining forest credits, in what was left of Indonesia and Congo, while the released option value of the desiccated Amazon created entirely different bubbles for a new generation of bright young things to make their fortunes on. That was part of the rise and fall, the natural rhythm of capital. Even then, with everything gone, Anders could have got back in the game. But something fundamental had changed. The Amazon crash spelled the end of that phase of multiplying possibilities that seemed to have no limitation, and expansion had been replaced by horse-trading over what was left. It was a new financial climate, one he did not understand. Once-dependable carbon stocks disappeared in a puff of smoke, species banks of least concern suddenly plunged into negative value, speculation grew ever more wild – things were not predictable. The baseline had skewed too far and he had not adapted.

Anders removed his shoes and his socks, spread his long toes on the lawn. The blades of grass tickled his feet. His generation had opened the world. No one could take that away from him. He stared at the lawn, his vision drifting from the nearest blades of grass to the grass that spread beyond his feet, softening and widening, speckled with lurid dandelions, until his focus slipped and all he could see was green. The effect felt a bit like going blind, or what he imagined might be the first second of the real-isation of blindness occurring. The greenness was entirely abstract, not a colour but a sensation – stripped of meaning, stripped of value. It was the outermost edge of panic. He held it as long as he could.

The garden came into focus again, dazzlingly sharp and defined. Nothing had changed. There was no going back. He watched the trees. He watched the light. He finished the last of the chocolate bar. The ache was behind his collarbones and the leaves were falling.

Life on the Planets

❧

When life on the planet became too unpleasant, its inhabitants fled to other worlds. Some left as nations, bearing flags, in fleets of ships that filled the sky like sparks from a kicked-up fire. Some left in hordes, out for plunder, but lost their bearings in the deafening upthrust of takeoff. Some left in sects, covering their ships in idols that burnt off as they passed through the atmosphere. Some left in political factions, chanting slogans at the stars, which diminished into atonal warbles the farther out they travelled. Some left gallantly, swaggering through orbit, mistaking empty space for freedom. Some slunk away ashamed, taking cover behind new moons where their old world wouldn't see them. Some left with their families and bickered over rations. Some left with other people's wives or husbands, venturing into erotic unknowns. Some stragglers left in twos and threes, sharing their stasis pods with strangers. Some lonely ones left with their cats and a lifetime's supply of kibble. Some left in cacophonous multitudes, some left in nervous swarms. Some just wandered out alone, their heads full of nothing.

Some settled on a mountainous world where the gravity was askew, and grew enormous bulbous heads and feet that trailed like weeds. Some settled on a world with colours none had ever seen before, and fell prey to violent new emotions and breakdowns of rational thought. Some settled on a putrescent planet whose core was a decaying ball, and their nostrils covered over with protective films. Some settled on a gas giant, and developed silver-winged balloons that billowed through the acid-green murk as if across an ocean. Some settled on a world with nine suns, and were followed by nine shadows. Some settled on a world of ash that plumed high above their heads, and communicated by choking. Some settled on a world of rain, where words like 'dry' and 'desiccation' vanished from their language. Some settled on a world of ice, and evolved to be shy and strange. Some settled across an asteroid belt, connecting their disparate chunks of rock with a perilous system of ladders. Some wild ones harnessed meteorites, and rode them bareback through the void. Some came across a space-capsule pointlessly orbiting a frozen sun, and lived their lives in nostalgic yearning for the photographs it contained. Some tuned in to old radio waves long-ago broadcast from their world, thought them transmissions from unknown aggressors, and scattered in terror through space. Some learned to live on suns, in protective bubbles of supercooled steel, and grew to look like furious insects with burnt matchstick heads. Some settled inside a black hole, and forgot themselves. Some didn't settle at all, but wandered forever between the stars in the hope of something better.

Some died in chemical reactions, melting into fantastical sludge that congealed into outlandish stalagmites. Some died in brilliant sublimations, bursting into light. Some spun freezing through the vacuum, watching the breath inside their visors bloom into flowers of ice. Some turned into fiery comets whose trails were the memories of former loves. Some were beaten to death by space-brutes. Some were bewitched by galactic perverts with thin lips and quivering fingers. Some were absorbed by sentient gases. Some wandered into perilous frequencies, and became pure sound. Some comprised the dust of new worlds. Some grew huge and sad, like clouds. Some giggled themselves to atoms.

The planet they had originally left shrivelled up like an old tangerine. Some ventured back, after countless years, but didn't linger long.

Fung's

❧

I drove past Fung's a few days ago. Of course, it isn't Fung's now. It's an empty building surrounded by weeds, an ugly breezeblock shell. There's plywood over the sliding doors and a spindly tree, or maybe an enormous weed, waving from the roof. The car-park contains a single shopping trolley, once painted green.

I slowed the car but there wasn't much to see. Even the sign has come off. I remembered when we erected those letters, me and Ranjeet, with Leena below: banging them up there one by one to spell F, FU, FUN, FUNG, FUNG'S. Perhaps they rotted and fell down like that, one at a time, beginning at the end. Undoing the name.

It hasn't been Fung's for fifteen years, but what other name could it have? Every place needs a name or else it's just dead space.

Of course, it was dead space before it was Fung's. Merely a different type of dead space. Somewhere that affected life and was all the more dead for trying. And now it's reverted to dead space again, and this time it's properly dead. But between those stretches of dead space, there was a period of time – it wasn't much more than a couple of months – when there was a flowering of wonderment. I lived through the glory days.

I drove past Fung's and then left it behind. I could have stopped, but what would have been the point? You can stop, but you can't go back.

❧

Mr Fung took over the Superway when I'd been working there for six months. He assembled all staff outside the walk-in meat fridge and delivered a short speech. 'I want to achieve big changes here,' he beamed. He was dressed in a Superway shirt and slip-on carpet shoes. 'I want to make this store a beacon. A true retail *experience*.'

No one reacted. The shelf-stackers glowered. The only sound was the slow *clack-clack* of gum.

'We start today,' he announced the next morning. I was getting ready on the deli counter, pulling on my sanitised gloves. 'The deli counter is closed,' he said. 'No customer access from aisles ten to fourteen. I want to move some things around. Things are going to look a bit different.' We exchanged glances. A doss, we imagined. But Mr Fung had other ideas.

The first thing he wanted us to do was to drag the deli counter out so it protruded at a right angle from the wall. It required ten members of staff to shift. In order to make space for this we had to reposition several aisles, which meant first removing all the products from the shelves. 'Stack them up against the back wall,' said Mr Fung. 'Customers will still want to buy these things, so let's try to create an orderly new zone.' But that wasn't easy. At nine the doors opened and customers began filtering in. They were quite confused. The supermarket looked like a construction site. 'We apologise for the inconvenience,' announced Mr Fung with a microphone at intervals throughout the morning, 'several aisles are temporarily closed as part of Superway's reorganisation. Feel free to look for the products you desire along the wall at the back of the store. Things will be back to normal soon, enjoy your Superway experience.'

'I want to get some biscuits,' a customer told me, gesturing bad-temperedly down the twelfth aisle. Access was blocked by a barricade of trolleys we'd erected where the shelving began, and members of staff were ferrying products to the growing heap by the wall.

'This aisle's closed today,' I said. 'Everything's getting moved around.'

'Why is this happening?' asked another. 'It's impossible to find anything.'

'Sorry, you'll have to look in that pile,' was all I could suggest.

'Good work,' said Mr Fung at the end of the day. The automatic doors were closed and the checkout assistants were cashing up. 'We've made a good start. You've all done well. Things look a lot less linear now.' He nodded approvingly down the shop floor, where aisles ten to fourteen had once stood. The symmetry of the aisles had gone. Aisles ten and eleven were positioned at right angles, and twelve and thirteen protruded diagonally, creating a confusion of planes. 'That's just the beginning,' he declared.

Over the course of the following week, under Mr Fung's direction, we systematically 'de-ordered' the remaining aisles, starting with aisles five to nine, then aisles one to four, and finally the various counters. By Saturday the shop floor was unrecognisable. Some of the aisles led to dead ends, and the positioning of others created small rooms to which access could only be gained through a narrow gap between shelves. The floor staff wandered these new lanes, trying to make sense of what we'd done. It was disorientating.

'Excellent,' said Mr Fung. We were gathered around him in a semi-circle, eating the chocolate ice-cream bars he'd handed out in appreciation of our efforts. 'I think this creates a much more interesting space. This will be a retail *experience*. Next week's job is getting products back on shelves. We can't expect our customers to root round in that pile forever.' He grinned and gave an exaggerated wink. None of us knew what to make of it.

On Monday morning, Mr Fung explained his plans for de-ordering the products. 'We'll mix things up a bit,' he said. He was wearing a shiny purple suit and casually tossing a tangerine from one hand to the other. 'Customers develop patterns, you know. They buy the same things time and again. They adopt certain habits. That's not good for retail diversity. That's not good for business.' He wandered over to the mountain of products heaped chaotically at the back, and gazed at it intently. 'Stack these according to taste,' he said. 'Salty things starting from the right hand side, spicy in the middle, sweet at the far left. There will obviously be some crossover zones, sweet and spicy being the most obvious example. Any questions about classification, ask me. Right, let's get started.'

No one moved or said a word. We were dumbfounded. Mr Fung regarded this inertia, then drew back the sleeve of his jacket and consulted his watch.

'It's four minutes past seven,' he said. 'We're open for business in two hours' time. By eight fifty-five, I want to see this Superway divided into those three declared zones: salty, spicy and sweet. It's a big job, what are you waiting for? Let's go!' And with this, he flung the tangerine directly at Tony, the surly eighteen year-old who usually worked at the fish counter. The fruit plumped into Tony's chest and splatted softly on the floor. Tony stared in disbelief. 'Let's *go*!' yelled Mr Fung again. There was no disagreeing with that.

The task was complex and ridiculous. There was no way we'd have finished it by nine. But it turned out that didn't really matter, because barely half an hour later, Mr Fung made another announcement.

'Okay, change of plan,' he cried, bounding down the aisle. 'I've been rethinking our marketing strategy. This division of products won't work. It's too simplistic. Customers won't like it. They'll think we're patronising them. I've also brainstormed a number of products that may present some difficulties – fall through the net, as it were.' He consulted a clipboard. 'Yeast, for example. So what we'll do instead is this: stack everything *alphabetically*.'

'Do what?' someone asked in disbelief.

'Start with the A products at the far left – almonds, anchovies, aniseed, aspirin – and work our way through the Bs and the Cs all the way down to Z. If we have any products beginning with Z. It's possible that we don't. This, I believe, is the most logical way to order the store. It will also be educational for junior customers. Any questions?'

Wasim, a balding shelf-stacker with a large Adam's apple and watery eyes, spoke up doubtfully. 'Are fruit and veg included in this? Do we put apples between… uh, anchovies and… uh, aspirin?'

'Fruit and veg are exempt for now. I've other plans for them.'

'How about refrigerated goods?' asked a grave-faced Slovakian girl called Leena.

'For now, refrigerated goods will fall under category F, for Frozen. Or perhaps under I for Icy, I'm not sure. Please consult me further on this when you get to the end of the Es.'

So we set to work. There were cynics among us. 'No fucking way this is going to work,' said Ranjeet, my fellow deli counter worker, in his habitually put-upon tone. 'I've worked in enough supermarkets, and I've never seen anything fucking like this. This is not how supermarkets go.'

'This is not how *most* supermarkets go,' said Mr Fung. He was standing behind us holding an economy tin of butter beans. His soft-soled shoes meant you couldn't hear him coming. Ranjeet and I both stepped back, eyeing the tin nervously. 'This, however, is not most supermarkets. This is a retail *experience*. In time, you will learn this,' He gave Ranjeet's arm an encouraging slap. Ranjeet looked even more unhappy.

When the clock went nine the doors were still closed, and I could see the faces of customers peering through the tinted glass. 'We're only on D,' Wasim explained when Mr Fung came back to take stock. 'We have to keep rearranging it all. We find another thing that starts with B, and we have to slide all the other products down.'

'We can't get this done. Not with customers in. I mean, no fucking way,' said Ranjeet.

'Okay, I'm taking a managerial decision,' announced Mr Fung. 'The store will not open today. We are closed for Alphabetisation. Things will be back to normal soon, we apologise for any inconvenience caused, but this is an important part of Superway's reorganisation.' He pointed at me. 'Go out and tell them this. Be polite but firm. Don't let them bully you. And then write a sign and stick it on the door.'

'Sorry, we're not open today,' I said to the people waiting outside. I only opened the door halfway in case one of them tried to squeeze through. 'We're closed for Alphabetisation. Things will be back to normal soon and we apologise for any inconvenience. It's an important part of Superway's reorganisation.'

'What's going on in there?' asked an old woman I recognised. 'Why have you done that with the aisles?'

'This is ridiculous,' said someone else. I gave them an apologetic smile and slipped back inside.

'You can't close a store down like this, man,' hissed Ranjeet disbelievingly, as we sifted through the product mountain for things starting with E. 'That's not how supermarkets work. It's just not something you can do.'

But, as we were starting to discover, Mr Fung could.

When we opened up again two days later, the Alphabetisation process was complete. Walking the aisles, already disordered, or 'de-linearised' as Mr Fung termed it, was a strange and bewildering experience. It went against every retail convention we'd ever known.

The various sections were demarcated by capital letters painted on cardboard in Superway's trademark lime green. Fish-counter Tony had painted the letters, and his calligraphy skills weren't good. The letters were drippy and badly composed. 'We'll get proper signs made up,' said Mr Fung when Leena complained they looked unprofessional. 'This is just a stop-gap, you know. Nothing is permanent. The important thing is to see what works. We learn by a process of trial and error. This store is a living experiment.'

But dissent was growing in certain quarters. There were those among the staff who objected to living experiments, or experiments of any kind at all. We were an unexperimental bunch, an assortment of cynical slackers and hard-working recent immigrants; for some this was essential employment for sending money home to their families, while others had nothing to spend their wages on but weed. If anything united us, it was the unquestioned assumption that employment in a Superway store could never turn out to be anything but a monotonous repetition of tasks. In other words steady, non-challenging work, with no shocks or surprises. And most of us quite liked it that way. There was a certain comfort in boredom. Living experiments weren't in the job description.

The first to jump ship were Gabby and Nicole, two best friends who worked on the tills, and whose names I could never get the right way round. They clearly had what Mr Fung later termed a 'low imagination threshold'. I assume the changes simply freaked them out. They didn't turn up for work one morning, and soon afterwards they were joined by Mike, who worked in the unloading bay, and a chubby stoner called Doff who suffered from a bad skin condition. From that point on, the Superway experienced a slow haemorrhaging of labour. Mr Fung didn't appear to mind, and never made any visible attempt to recruit extra staff. 'This is what we call a streamlining process,' he said, in one of his morning meetings, when Wasim pointed out the fact we no longer had any security guards. 'This store is downsizing. Re-evaluating. And anyway, we don't really need security at present.'

This was true. The doors had been closed for a week while other changes were implemented. Mr Fung had ordered carpets to be laid down the length of each aisle, to give the shop-floor a more 'tactile' feel, and drapes to be hung from the ceiling to make the place 'cosy'. Following his emotive tirade against the strip-lights which made the store 'like one of those places you identify corpses', we had also spent several days fitting incandescent bulbs and rigging up paper shades to diffuse their glare. It did not matter to Mr Fung that none of us were qualified to rewire electric lights. He provided overalls, directing the proceedings from a swivel chair he had wheeled from his office to the middle of the store. Occasionally he leapt up from this throne to patrol the evolving aisles, stopping now and then to scribble notes in his pad. His ideas changed rapidly and without warning, and it wasn't unusual for a team to spend an entire morning on one task, only to dismantle it after lunch. But Mr Fung was exuberant. His enthusiasm was boundless. And the more his detractors fell away, the more his strange zeal came to affect those of us who remained.

'He's out of his mind. He's wrong in the head,' said Ranjeet one evening after work, after he had spent the whole day painting the trolleys green to make them look 'less like cages'. 'I'm telling you, man, it's too fucking weird. If it goes on like this much longer, I'm getting out.' But I could tell that – like most of those who remained, who weathered the desertions in our ranks and stayed to work at the Superway through its various incarnations – he was secretly fascinated.

Already, in those early days, I think a few of us were starting to see Mr Fung for what he really was. A retail visionary.

He took me aside a few mornings later, the moment I got to work. I don't know why he singled me out, but he appeared to have it all planned. He was wearing a different suit that day, a slightly louder shade of purple, along with a truly hideous veined purple tie.

'What's your usual position in this store?' he asked. 'I mean, before.'

'I normally work at the deli counter.'

'*Deli*,' he muttered, as if he hadn't thought of that. He looked startled and worried for a second. But then his face brightened again. He had taken me by the elbow, and was guiding me towards the front of the store, where the sliding doors were located. 'Well you won't be at the deli any more. In fact, we may not even have a deli. I want you to be in charge of organising the garden.'

'The garden?' I asked, confused.

'Tell me, when a customer enters a supermarket, any supermarket, in any country, what is the first thing he sees?'

'Newspapers. Magazines. Fruit and veg.'

'Correct. And why does he see fruit and veg?'

'Because it's green and fresh. It makes the place feel healthy.'

'Exactly, yes. Green and fresh. And this Superway store will adhere to that principle. There are some conventions that can't be changed. However, they can be *improved, re-imagined*. Where does fruit and veg come from?'

'Where does it come from? Lots of places.'

'I'm speaking fundamentally,' he said, snapping his fingers impatiently. 'Does it come from a factory? Out of a tin?'

'Uh, from trees, bushes, the ground…'

'Exactly right,' beamed Mr Fung. We had reached the fruit and veg shelves now – they were empty, having been bare for a week, with only a few root vegetables and wilted stalks to show what they had been before

– where he gestured expansively. 'You think our customers want to see these green, fresh things on those plastic shelves, in those temperature-controlled compartments, under those glaring lights?'

I shook my head. He was staring at me. I couldn't imagine what he wanted. He unfolded several sheets of paper covered in diagrams.

'These,' he said proudly, holding them before me, 'are my plans for Fruit Eden.'

I stared at the paper. It was incomprehensible.

'Fruit Eden?' I asked.

'That is how it will be known. The concept is based, loosely, on the Hanging Gardens of Babylon.'

I studied the papers in more detail. The plans looked entirely improbable. From what I could tell from the 'artist's impression', oranges, apples, bananas and melons were clustered together in some sort of steaming tropical forest. There was a meadow of salad leaves, a kind of Japanese rock garden bristling with herbs, and what appeared to be a waterfall cascading down one of the walls.

'This is only provisional,' Mr Fung said, as if sensing my doubt. 'The exact details of the plans may change in the execution.'

'And I'm in charge of this?' I asked.

'I'm giving you full control.'

'And how… how do I make this stuff?'

'It's up to you to implement the vision in the way you see fit. I've been watching you work. I trust your abilities. You must use all the materials at your disposal, and hand-pick a small team of assistants from among the staff. It is my intention that Fruit Eden will be one of this store's greatest assets, a true retail *experience*. You have two weeks to complete the project, after which time the doors will reopen to the public. Any questions?'

Dumbly, I just shook my head. I didn't know what else to do.

For my team I selected Leena, because I liked her seriousness, Ranjeet, to get him off painting trolleys, and a Kurdish guy I barely knew called Kaseem, because I liked his face. I also picked surly Tony, who, against all expectations, had stuck it out against Mr Fung's occasional tangerine assaults, and appeared surprisingly unfazed by the store's gradual slide into madness. Tony seemed a good solid type, and proved to be useful when it came to hammer-work and heavy lifting. We had our first meeting later that day, smoked a pack of cigarettes between us, cordoned off the proposed work area, and dragged the old shelves into storage.

That afternoon, using the expense account Mr Fung had given us, I ordered twenty bags of concrete, five rolls of Astroturf, ten tarpaulins, thirty metres of hose, twelve bags of soil and twelve bags of fertiliser. The next morning, Ranjeet and I drove to the nearby garden centre in a home delivery van to load up with ivy, ferns, assorted creepers and vines, a dozen rubber plants, ten banana trees, and as many potted herbs as we could stuff into the racks. We spent whatever money was left on orchids and Venus fly-traps. The bill ran into the thousands of pounds. Mr Fung wanted no receipts.

Fruit Eden evolved haphazardly. We had no idea what we were doing. Tony and Kaseem had both had previous jobs on building sites, so all the concrete and structural work was their responsibility. By the end of the fourth day, they had constructed two large ponds and a monstrous concrete feature, which was supposed to look like rocks for the cascading waterfall. Ranjeet and I tried to get it working, running hosepipes up the wall, but the water came out in a pathetic trickle so we decided to cut shelves into it and turn it into 'Citrus Rock', which would display lemons, limes and oranges and be festooned with bougainvillaea. Instead of a waterfall we had to settle for a couple of dribbling fountains. The concrete ponds we filled with water lilies, on which could be balanced small plastic signs informing customers of important price reductions.

The five of us came to enjoy a celebrity status in the store. Select groups of the other employees were engaged on several notable side-projects, but most were still slugging away at the seemingly endless re-categorisation of products. Mr Fung had had doubts about Alphabetisation, and for three days had become obsessed with what he called 'Full Product Spectrum', or sometimes 'Consumer Rainbow'. His new idea was to display everything according to colour. The left-hand side of the store would be red, and then orangey-red products would give way to an orange section, which would blend seamlessly into yellows, following the colour spectrum through greens, blues and purples into blacks, against the right-hand wall.

Or at least, this was the idea. It didn't prove popular. The prospect of taking all the products off the shelves again and putting them back in yet another order caused a minor rebellion among the staff. There was a rash of further walk-outs. At first people refused to get involved, and when they did, they did the job badly, so it was less a Consumer Rainbow than a mish-mash of different colour patches, the result of which sent Mr Fung into a rage. It was the first time, I think, that anyone had seen him angry. He stormed off into the loading bay, cursing furiously to himself, and remained in there for several minutes. When he came back, to the amazement of everyone, he publicly recanted. 'I've brainstormed the Full Colour Spectrum, and concluded the concept will not be adopted by this Superway store. After careful consideration, I've decided the rainbow effect may well prove distressing to some customers. There are certain psychological effects that cannot fully be predicted – people getting angry in the reds, or nauseous in the yellows. Aisles of unbroken grey might create depression. In light of such risks to mental health, the process of re-Alphabetisation will begin forthwith.'

Critics of Mr Fung used this speech as evidence that he lacked any overall vision, that he was growing confused and indecisive. His supporters said it showed that he was listening to his workers' concerns, that he was not the maverick egotist his detractors made him out to be. Further rifts began to grow among what remained of the staff, from which those of us employed on Fruit Eden were happily exempt. We were working on a higher project, something with grandeur and scale. We didn't need to involve ourselves in these petty intrigues. Our exclusivity didn't make us popular, however: there were rumours we were being paid more, that we enjoyed special privileges.

By the end of two weeks, our Fruit Eden looked like a half-built theme park. We asked for more time. We were given four days. We worked flat out for the whole period, staying after work until midnight to finish laying Astroturf, spreading fertiliser over the beds, pressing flowers into the moist soil. Tony really took to this. He had never planted anything before. Gradually, unbelievably, the project came together. Mr Fung spun in his swivel chair, checking his charts and surveying our work, until we finally put down our tools and left at the end of the night.

In all the time I worked for him, I never saw Mr Fung leave the store. There were rumours that he slept in his office on a bed made of packing crates, but these stories were never confirmed, because no one had ever been in there.

On the morning of the grand opening, we stocked the shelves with produce. In several areas we had borrowed from Mr Fung's Full Product Spectrum concept, and Leena had created gorgeous displays of fresh fruit.

Citrus Rock was spectacular, rising from lemon yellow at the bottom, through diffusive grapefruit tones, into topmost shades of deep blood-orange red. It looked like a thermometer about to burst. Other fruit was clustered together into something that loosely resembled the original jungle plans, bananas, pineapples and melons displayed in a glistening forest of green leaves. The herb garden looked pretty shabby, but I was confident it would improve with nurturing. Leena's main addition to the project was the creation of the 'Lettuce Meadow', an expanse of salad leaves arranged across a wide sloping area, access to which could be gained by a narrow wooden bridge.

The last things to go in were several industrial humidifiers, which had raised the cost of the project by another few thousand pounds. They covered the area in a fine mist. It was like being in a tropical greenhouse. The disadvantage of the humidifiers was that anyone entering Fruit Eden got soaked to the skin in seconds, but we planned to supply waterproof ponchos for customers to use free of charge.

Mr Fung announced the grand opening over the loudspeakers. Today, he said, was the culmination not only of the Fruit Eden project, but the 're-imagining' process that had taken place across the whole store, from the Alphabetisation of the shelves to Fish World and the Frozen North, right through to the bloody spectacle of Meat Zone. He congratulated all remaining staff, those of us who had stuck it out, who had not shied away from experimentation or faltered at new ideas. Tomorrow, he declared, the doors would reopen, and 'a new supermarket paradigm' would at last be unleashed on the world.

Mr Fung popped a bottle of Cava and raised his plastic cup to Fruit Eden. The humidifiers steamed up the glasses on his face, mist condensed on his forehead. We watched him, anxiously, for an opinion. He appeared absolutely delighted, almost childishly happy.

After a short opening ceremony, in which Mr Fung had donned a poncho, crossed the bridge over Lettuce Meadow, plucked an apple from the Tree of Knowledge – this, surprisingly, was Tony's inspiration, an ungainly concrete construction enwrapped by a serpent made of painted hosepipes – and taken a ceremonial bite, the staff were encouraged to spend time wandering around the store, in order to familiarise ourselves with new developments. I stuck with my team, each of us swigging from a miniature bottle of white wine, which Mr Fung had distributed from a loaded trolley. We saw

the Frozen North, the icy bunker that comprised the new frozen foods de-
partment, and had a look at Fish World, which was unpleasant. We sat down
on the sofas, armchairs and chaise-longues that had appeared along some
of the aisles, to provide 'calm spots' whenever customers grew fatigued. We
explored the bewildering labyrinth of shelves, which had changed shape
four or five times since I had last been involved, and made even more disorientating by the erection of screens and the hanging of curtains, all part of
Mr Fung's self-declared 'war on linearity'.

'What about security?' Wasim had asked several weeks before.

'Security?' said Mr Fung, as if he scorned the word.

'I mean, CCTV cameras and stuff. How will we see the shoplifters
now? There are blind spots everywhere, all over the store.' Wasim, despite
his permanent expression of fear intermingled with doubt, was one of
those loyal employees who had stuck it out.

In response, Mr Fung had told a surprising story.

'After the revolutions in France, the government redesigned Paris. All
the new roads were built in straight lines, a bit like conventional supermarkets. Do you know why? To give cannons a clear line of fire. That's the
same principle behind security cameras. To give them a clear line of fire, to
eliminate blind spots.'

The assembled staff were puzzled and impressed. At times like these,
I had the sense that Mr Fung was hinting at something that went beyond
new retail experiences and supermarket paradigms. As if he was revealing
something hidden.

'Do we want to create that sort of store?' Mr Fung went on. 'A
supermarket founded on fear of the very people it serves?'

'But what about the shoplifters?' asked Wasim, standing with his
mouth slightly open.

To this, Mr Fung had said nothing.

We finished our miniature bottles of wine and pushed Tony around
in one of the trolleys that Ranjeet had painted green. We practised locat-
ing products under the Alphabetisation system, in preparation for the
opening next day. It wasn't as straightforward as it sounded. It was hard to
guess, for example, whether a bar of milk chocolate would appear under C
for chocolate, M for milk chocolate, or even B for bar. People had told Mr
Fung of these concerns. He'd called them 'teething problems'.

My team wandered off. It was dark outside. All the lights were blazing in the store. I kissed Leena when we were alone, in one of the rooms created by the positioning of aisles. It was a hasty, clumsy thing, and both of us laughed afterwards. We were surrounded by L-products: lager, lard, lasagne sheets, lemonade, lipstick, Listerine, lollipops. I tried to sit her in her own shelf space, between leashes and leggings.

'This is one of those blind spots,' I said, putting my lips against her neck. I don't know if she got the reference. I thought it would seem embarrassing later, but it never did.

We resumed trading the next morning. The doors to reality opened.

The reopening hadn't been advertised, so it took a long time before any customers actually came. Mr Fung greeted them at the door. He was wearing his purple suit, with a red bougainvillea flower in the lapel. He shook their hands, welcomed them to the store, and personally handed them a shopping basket or matched them up with a trolley. 'Take your time,' he said. 'Make yourself at home.'

The customers entered cautiously, with a look of trepidation. The first thing they encountered was Fruit Eden. The humidifiers were on full blast, and before long the condensation built up and dripped from the ceiling like rain, which we hadn't anticipated. We had to hand out umbrellas to go with the waterproof ponchos. Despite these protections, few of the customers actually ventured over the bridge that spanned Lettuce Meadow. They were not adventurous. Some picked lemons from Citrus Rock, but to get to the ruby grapefruit and blood oranges they had to climb twelve feet up a ladder, and none of them attempted that. They dithered at the edges and stared. They wiped perspiration from their foreheads. 'It looks nice, I guess,' one man said. But nobody else said anything.

From there they entered into the aisles, following the alphabet. Tony's sloppy letter signs had been replaced with smarter ones, printed in the Superway green on plastic notices, but they still seemed to find the system confusing. They constantly had to ask where things were. They seemed upset by the lack of straight lines, and half of the little rooms remained unexplored. They came upon darkly watchful employees positioned at every junction, staring at them to see how they reacted.

The wheels of their trolleys caught on the carpets. Some of them got hopelessly lost. They kept knocking things off the shelves. There was mounting exasperation.

At the end of the day, when the last of them had found their way back and been ushered out, the sales on the tills were disappointing. We'd received sixteen complaints, with one man threatening to sue over slipping on the wet floor at Fruit Eden. Comments included 'disorientating', 'nightmarish and Kafkaesque', 'an impossible environment to shop in', and 'a revolting joke'. This last was a comment about Meat Zone, which seemed to have caused quite a stir.

'Teething problems,' said Mr Fung, in his subsequent debriefing. We were gathered around the tills, passing round the packet of biscuits he had handed out. 'Of course it takes time for new ideas to filter through to the public. They have never seen anything like this before. They are overwhelmed. The more revolutionary the concept the harder it is to comprehend.' He appeared defiant and up-beat, hopping round energetically and beaming at us all. He assured us that sales would pick up, that customers would come flocking before long.

At the end of the first week, as customer footfall increased slightly, Mr Fung was still confident enough to initiate a new rota system he called 'Staff Switcheroo'. The idea, he explained, was to counter monotony creeping in as we all settled down to our regular jobs, now that the excitement of the reorganisation was over. He didn't want us to grow despondent. He didn't want a workforce of automatons, he said. Throughout the day, at intervals of between fifteen minutes and two hours, an announcement would be broadcast overhead: 'All staff switch, all staff switch, with immediate effect. Thank you.' Upon hearing this, all employees would immediately move to a new position: check-out staff would turn into shelf-stackers, shelf-stackers would man Fish World, Fish World servers would collect trolleys, trolley attendants would rush to the loading bay. We carried laminated sheets that told us the order of duties.

We did a trial run before opening, and everything went quite smoothly. But when the customers were in, the changeovers became chaotic. People would complain about shop attendants charging off in the middle of helping them track down some product beginning with J, sometimes leaving halfway through a sentence. An elderly woman was almost knocked over in the rush to get through the aisles. 'Things will settle down,' said Mr Fung. 'After a few weeks, Switcheroo will become so effortless you can do it blindfolded.' He frowned, thinking for a moment, and it wouldn't have surprised me if he'd whipped out blindfolds there and then. But he turned away.

At the end of that month, Mr Fung's smile no longer came so easily.

His feet had lost their bounce. Things were going badly wrong, despite the reassurances and pep talks he gave us in the morning meetings, which even some of his loyal supporters had started to call propaganda. Sales, which had initially picked up following that first 'teething' week, were falling. We took less every trading day. Our regular customers had deserted us. New customers came once, sometimes even twice, but not again. The only regulars we managed to attract were a collection of mad old tramps, who came to put their feet up on the chaise-longues or wander the aisles for the afternoon, smiling happily to themselves, picking things up and putting them down again.

Either it's a tribute to Mr Fung's inclusiveness, his generous soul, that he didn't have these itinerates thrown out, or a mark of his desperation.

Employees continued to fall by the wayside. Even those who Mr Fung had inspired, those who had initially glimpsed his bright new dawn. We were down to a skeleton staff. Me, Ranjeet, Tony, Wasim, Leena and a score of irregulars. Kaseem had quietly vanished a week ago. And then Tony quit as well. He said he had to study for exams, but I lost all respect for him.

'You're not going to quit, are you?' I asked Ranjeet one day, after he'd been bitching about the long hours and the fact we were still on the minimum wage.

'Quit?' he said. 'I don't quit, man. I'm not quitting smoking, and I'm not quitting Fung's.'

This, I think, was the first time that anyone had called it this. Out loud, at any rate. Perhaps we'd all begun to give it this name in our minds long ago. He was right: it wasn't Superway now. It was Fung's. There could be no other name.

I still kissed Leena from time to time. On the bridge over Lettuce Meadow, or in the chaos of the Switcheroo. She'd write a single letter on the back of a receipt and we'd meet in the Gs or the Ks or the Ns, rush through the motions of a brief, fumbled tryst, and then hurry back to our duties.

But Fung's plunged deeper into problems by the day. It was a sinking ship. We'd practically gutted and rebuilt the place in a couple of inspired weeks, and now our deficiencies in design, planning, construction, engineering, electronics, hydraulics and everything else were becoming apparent. Fish World stank. Almost no one could enter. The Frozen North was in crisis. There was some problem with temperature control, and ice now covered the walls and floor, with icicles starting to grow down from the ceiling. Chisels had to be provided to hack away rock-hard sausages that had become embedded in the walls, like prehistoric hunters. Meat Zone was another liability. Children had run howling from the sight. There was blood seeping through one of the walls, and no one could work out where it was coming from.

By the end of a fortnight, it was clear that even Fruit Eden was failing. Digging out wilted produce and getting fresh stuff onto the shelves proved to be a laborious business, and with the staff shortage and the constant Switcheroos the job wasn't being done properly. The area was nearly impossible to clean. Decomposing matter built up in the cracks. The bright hues of Citrus Rock slowly faded from yellow to brown, and Lettuce Meadow turned into a sodden swamp. Dark shadows of damp appeared on the walls, and the humidifiers had to be decommissioned. Clouds of fruit flies circled above, despite the Venus fly-traps.

The worst thing was the change in Mr Fung. We watched as his energy drained away, with occasional resurgences of zeal, the fervour repossessing him, sometimes for hours at a time, and then dissipating again. The vigorous speeches became less frequent. He no longer threw things at people. He spent more time sitting in his swivel chair, gazing at the slow train-wreck of his store, turning circles with his feet. Just going round and round.

We all waited for the next big idea, the next doomed, inspirational scheme to get things moving, to turn things around, to check the steady rot. We would have gone along with it, too, we who stayed with him to the end. We would have followed any crazed vision, even if – perhaps especially if – we knew it could only fail. It would have been worth it just to see the old eagerness filling him again, his face lighting up like a fridge when the door has been thrown open.

But after a certain point the big ideas stopped coming.

It happened one day shortly after closing, when the tills were being emptied of their miserable takings, the lights switched off in the grottoes of Fruit Eden. It was Wasim who opened the doors, apprehending that the two men outside, the two men with the suits and the briefcase, were not customers arriving late but a portent of something else. Something official. They were both tall, clean and polite. They asked to see the manager. We led them towards the office. I could see their eyes flicking around as we navigated them through the aisles, but the expressions on their faces never altered. I was the one who opened the door, and I tried to see if there was a bed made of packing crates in there, but all I could see was a desk with files and folders on it.

Mr Fung received the men with a calm, accepting smile. He shook their hands and stepped aside, then closed the door. There was something embarrassing about the glimpse I had of him, just before the office door closed. He suddenly looked ridiculous, smiling away in an ugly purple suit that was slightly too large, a wilted flower in the lapel. I felt a rush of shame.

'That's it. He's in the shit now,' said Ranjeet, half an hour later. The office door was still closed. None of us had left.

'Why do you say that?' asked Leena. She was sitting on my knee. It wasn't very comfortable; she was a bony girl.

'I reckon they're the guys who own the franchise. They're the guys from Superway.' He was sitting at a cash register and smoking, knocking the ash into one of the empty drawers.

The two men left after half an hour. When their car had gone, the car-park was empty. We waited for another fifteen minutes to see if Mr Fung would come out, but he stayed in his office. It didn't seem right to disturb him.

The next morning he made a short speech. This Superway store was closing, he said. He was stepping down as manager. It was not economically viable. He hoped it would reopen soon under different management, so we could keep our jobs. He was sorry things hadn't worked out. And he wished he could give us some compensation, to last until things were back to normal, but there was no money available.

'That's it?' said Wasim. His Adam's apple went up and down. I thought he was about to cry.

'Yes. That's it,' said Mr Fung.

'What about everything we've done?' demanded Ranjeet furiously.

'There's nothing more to do,' said Mr Fung. 'This store is perfect, in every way.' He smiled sadly. 'I'm very, very proud.'

The doors didn't open that day. Or ever again, for that matter. I don't know if Superway planned to reopen under new management, to wipe away everything we'd done and return things to the way they were, but with the economic situation and the general pattern of closures nationwide, I suppose the odds were against it. I'm glad, of course, it has been this way. I'm glad that nothing came after. Given that the Superway brand itself went bust about a year later, laying off thousands of staff across the country, it might seem, to a fantasist, almost a vindication. But history has no jurisdiction to vindicate men like Mr Fung. He needs no one's approval.

It was Ranjeet who suggested it, although he said it as a joke. It was me who took the idea up and made us follow it through. We got to work that afternoon, the last afternoon we spent at Fung's, cutting the letters from balsa wood with a hacksaw in the car-park. We painted them lime green with the paint that Tony had used for his letter signs. Then we got a ladder and climbed to the flat, gravelled roof.

It was hard to get the old sign off, but we managed it with a mallet and a crowbar. There was no risk in cutting the wires, because the electricity had been disconnected earlier that day. Under our feet, the fruit flies were swarming over the rot of Fruit Eden; the Frozen North was melting now, loosening its grip on the sausages. We sent the Superway sign crashing down in three broken pieces to the concrete below. Leena let out a scream and jumped around. There was no one else to applaud or cheer. No one to witness the final switcheroo.

We banged the letters into place with nails, right into the wall. F, FU, FUN, FUNG, FUNG'S. There was no way to light them up, of course, but they stood out brightly, lime green on grey-black. Then we went to find Mr Fung.

He stood there for a long time, gazing at the sign. There was no expression on his face at all. He wiped his glasses, put them back on, and nodded his approval. Leena laughed. So did Ranjeet. Myself and Mr Fung remained silent.

Finally we followed him inside, back into the unilluminated store.

'Take what you want,' was the last thing he said. 'Anything. It's all yours.'

But we didn't really feel like taking much, in the end.

I never saw Wasim again. I imagine he's doing okay. I hung out with Ranjeet for a while, but we started to annoy each other, and after I went to university we lost all contact. All we had ever talked about was Fung's, and when there wasn't anything else about Fung's left to talk about, we didn't have much to say. I saw Leena on and off that summer. She got a job in a greengrocer's. I have no idea what became of her. She was the first girl who let me touch her breasts.

And where did Mr Fung go then? What's he doing now? I've asked around. No one seems to know. He wasn't the kind of man you keep in touch with.

Was he married? Did he have a family? Where did he even come from? No one seems to know that either. Sometimes I wish I'd talked to him, asked him more questions.

The story of Mr Fung's Superway has since become a textbook case of mismanagement at a senior level, of doomed retail strategy. It is studied in business studies seminars, held up as an extreme example of how a franchise can go badly wrong if chains of command are not adhered to and oversight not maintained. Middle managers talk about 'doing a Fung'. Consumer watchdogs use it to explain the collapse of accountability structures. Health and safety panels do slideshows about it, pointing out the lack of fire extinguishers and flagrant disregard for safety signs.

Those little men, those little women. I can only pity them. I know how it really was. I lived through the glory days.

I drove past Fung's a few days ago. Of course, it isn't Fung's now. I drove past Fung's and then left it behind. I could have stopped, but what would have been the point? You can stop, but you can't go back.

Vault of the Wordmonger

❧

Our father bought words once a week. He was a big man in our town and fresh words gave him status. He paid for them in animal parts from the farm our family owned and sometimes in mineral parts from the mine beyond the hill. He did not own the mine but he had interests there. The animal parts and mineral parts he carried there in his hands and the words he carried back in his mouth. That is the way to carry words. When I say back I mean he carried them back to the house in which we lived. It was a large house with pillars and a garden. When I say there I mean to the wordmonger which is where the words came from. I do not know how it was in your town but that was how it was in mine.

The wordmonger had her shop at the bottom of the hill and we lived at the top. Not at the very top of course but close enough to matter. This meant that our father carried the words back uphill which meant that he was out of breath by the time he reached our house. He could not use the words straight away or they would come out broken. All of us would gather around waiting for him to speak the words. By us I mean myself and my sister and my brother and my other brother. Our father would speak the words and we would wonder at their shapes. Their rounded bits and their curves. Their hard sounds and their edges. Then he would speak them again with a bit more confidence. Sometimes he would shout them. Later that night he would take his words to the place where other big men drank and he would demonstrate their use. A crowd would grow around him. I felt lucky as a child to have a father who could buy fresh words when he felt like it. I hoped to grow up like him.

A lot of time has gone by now and I can hardly remember the way he looked apart from his teeth and his moustache.

If he caught us using his words he would beat us with a shovel.

Occasionally he let me or my brother or my other brother go with him down the hill. He never let my sister. I was proud to walk with our father down the hill and through the streets with all the people watching us. We went past the salvage yards and over the dried river. The wordmonger had her shop on the other side of the wall which some people did not consider to be a part of our town at all but rather some other place. There were other shops down there selling things that I did not understand the uses of or what they were. The people looked different there but I cannot tell you how.

The shop was a building made of bricks that looked as if it had been built for a purpose that was not a shop but which no one remembered now. Its walls were painted green. The sign that hung above the door showed the lips of a mouth with lines flowing out of it wriggling here and there. I always liked that sign because it had a meaning. There were other signs in our town whose meanings were unknowable such as two crossed lines or an animal with four legs or a stick with a line through it or other things I did not understand. I do not think that anyone in our town understood them. The door of the shop was closed if the wordmonger was away but normally it was open and our father would walk straight in. The wordmonger would be waiting standing behind the counter.

She was not an old woman but the effect of her was old. Her hands were old and her hair was old but the rest of her was younger. She had a creased face like a piece of picked fruit and a dent above her nose as if someone had pushed it in. Her eyes were small and squinty. There was nothing inside the room but the counter and the booth and a long dark space behind. There were shelves and boxes there which was where she kept things.

Our father would place the animal parts or the mineral parts on the counter and she would take a look at them. She would pick them up and feel the weight of them in her hands and sniff the surfaces of them and look underneath them. Then she would disappear into the long dark space taking the parts with her and we would hear the sound of drawers scraping and doors opening. During this we would have to wait. Sometimes it took a minute and sometimes it took much longer. I suppose the length of time it took depended somehow on the words but I was never able to work out how. Our father would close his eyes as if he was sleeping.

The booth was a sort of wooden box with an entrance on each side.

I imagined it was very old but I had no way of knowing. When the word-monger returned she would go in one side and our father would go in the other side and sit down on a little stool. We were not supposed to look but sometimes we looked sideways. Between them in the wooden wall were lots of small square holes and our father would put his ear to the holes and she would put her mouth to the holes and speak softly into them. This is how the words were exchanged. This is how he received them. When his ear was full of words he would rise to his feet and brush his knees and say thank you to the wordmonger. I never heard him say it to anyone else but he said it to her. Then we would leave the shop and walk back up the hill. We were not allowed to speak to our father on the journey home.

Normally he was pleased and often his lips would be practising the shapes of the words silently. When he had a difficult word in his mouth he would frown. Occasionally the words he received were ones that he already knew or ones he did not know the uses for and he would be disappointed. But he never attempted to take them back or to complain to the wordmonger no matter how disappointed he was. Our father would argue with anyone but he did not argue with her.

People would stand aside as he walked back up the hill. They knew he was full of words and they did not want to spill them. The only person who was not respectful was the skinny old man who begged outside the salvage yards on his hands and knees. He was from the older time when words were not approved of. When he saw our father coming he would spit at him or make crude signs and our father would react or not depending on his mood. Sometimes he would kick the old man or try to step on his hands but mostly he ignored him. The old man was wordless and not worth the trouble.

Through the years of my childhood and my early adulthood I watched our father grow with words. He swelled and glowed with them. The outside of him did not change except in the usual ways but the inside of him changed in ways no one could see. There were thousands of words in there stored up ready to be used. Even if he did not know their uses they gave him power. Even if he never spoke them but kept them inside himself they still made him powerful. Perhaps even more so that way. Because he had so many words he was admired by everyone apart from the old beggar man who hardly counted as a man. He was admired by the bigger men who lived further up the hill. They came to him for advice and to help them make decisions and to have around them while they drank and played their games.

Our father said that one day his children would receive his words. Before he died he would give them to us dividing them equally. By us I mean myself and my brother and my other brother but not my sister because some words were not considered right for her. In my mind I planned to share them with her anyway. This was a great inheritance but it never came to pass. All we had to do was wait but unfortunately we did not.

𝔁

It was my other brother who came up with the idea. Not my brother but my other brother who was the youngest one. The idea did not come from nowhere but from the beating he received after our father caught him using one of his words. I do not know which word it was because I did not hear it. All I heard was the sound of the shovel thumping on my brother's legs and on his backside and on his back and his crying afterwards. When he had finished crying he came in search of me.

He did not want to wait for our father to be almost dead before he got his words. He wanted his own words now. His idea was to follow the wordmonger when she left her shop and went into the dead woods which she had been observed to do. He thought that she must know a place where words were just lying around for anyone to pick up. He would help himself. Once he had got words of his own he planned to leave our family home and marry the girl he was in love with lower down the hill. The word he had been beaten for was stolen to impress this girl but it did not mean what he thought it did. She had only laughed at him.

We chose a day when our father was out counting animal parts on the farm and we knew he would not be back until the evening. The two of us went down the hill and over the dried river. The door of the shop was open which meant that the wordmonger was inside. We waited there for several hours but no one left or entered. The day was hot and there was no shade in the area beyond the wall and we were thinking of going home when the wordmonger appeared. She locked the door of her shop and went off down the road.

My other brother followed her and I followed my other brother. We walked past the empty buildings and the rusted old machines and across the charcoal fields until we reached the dead woods. Neither myself nor my other brother had been there more than once or twice and we did not like it there. Everything was black and grey and there was no smell. We followed her along a path that led to another path that led to another path that led to another path. She walked ahead not looking back and we walked behind. At last we came to a place where the dead woods ended at a wall of grey rock. At the bottom of the rock there was a door. It was not normal sized but very tall and wide and it was not made of wood but of rusted metal. Its size did not matter though as it was not completely closed. There was a gap.

The wordmonger approached this gap without once looking back to see if she had been followed and slipped into the darkness.

Myself and my other brother waited for a while and when she did not come out we went a little closer. The wall was not made of rock but of something smooth and grey that was as hard as rock. I had seen this stuff before but only in small pieces. On the door was a sign that showed an open mouth like the sign above her shop. But instead of random lines coming from the mouth there were pictures we recognised. There was a human figure with a line going through its body and there were black flames and there was a skull.

Vault. The word was vault. I knew this from our father. We had heard of places like this but only in the stories. We were not supposed to listen but sometimes we listened sideways. When the big men drank too much they talked about the older time when words were not allowed. They were not allowed because of the bad things they had done. Words had caused a great fire or perhaps many fires and words had caused the sea to spill and drown the towns and buildings. Words had caused some men and women to kill other men and women and the other men and women to kill other men and women. Most of the animals had gone and words had caused that too. I did not understand exactly how words had done these things but for years afterwards they were kept away from us. They were hidden in deep holes and doors were closed upon them. These holes were called vaults and this was one of them. The pictures coming from the mouth were threats like our father's shovel.

Perhaps we would have gone inside or perhaps we would have gone away. I do not know because we heard her footsteps coming back. My other brother hopped about breathing very fast and picked up a piece of rock and put it behind his back. I stood beside the door. Something filled the dark gap and we saw the wordmonger. She had not noticed us. Her mouth was moving as if she was working at the shape of a new word. Or perhaps she was out of breath from where she had gone. As she stepped into the light she saw us both standing there. Her small squinty eyes went smaller and more squinty. She opened her mouth to speak but she never spoke because my other brother hit her with the rock.

She fell without a sound and lay there without moving. My other brother threw the rock away but it was done. Perhaps he expected words to spill out so that he could pick them up. But the only thing that spilled out was red and sticky.

We waited for something else to happen and when nothing else happened it was like a sign. We both turned different ways. My other brother took the path back into the dead woods and I went through the rusted door into the vault.

A lot of time has gone by now and I do not remember everything well. There was a hill inside the earth going down to somewhere deeper. At the bottom of the hill there was another rusted door and it was open like the first. Rocks had been pushed into the gap to keep it open. I wondered if the wordmonger had pushed the rocks in there or if it had been someone else. Someone from long ago perhaps. But everything was dusty and there was no way of knowing.

Past the second rusted door was a pit with smooth walls. It went down to a depth so deep I could not see its bottom. There was a hard confusing sound rising up inside the pit. It sounded as if a storm was trapped inside the earth. But it was not a storm. It was words. They were flying around down there bouncing off the walls and bouncing off each other and smashing into little bits and joining up again. Something had unleashed them from their trap and they were loose. I wondered when they had escaped. Maybe it was years ago. Maybe it was years and years. No one knew that they were there apart from the wordmonger and me. Now the wordmonger was dead it was only me.

I lay down on my front and looked into the pit. I thought that there were stars down there but they were little lights. They went bright and then dark and then bright again. There were also bigger things like pale glowing squares. The glowing squares were in the walls and across the front of them passed spiky lines going up and down and up and down. When the words got louder the lines got spikier like knives. I knew that I was seeing the secret shapes of words.

A great excitement came to me. I never knew that words had shapes. I knew that they had sound shapes but not seeing shapes. If I understood the shapes then I might understand the words.

Then an excitement came that was even greater than before. If I understood the shapes then I might know how words were made. I could make new words. Words that were my own.

With this excitement in my head I walked around the pit. On the other side of it were bars sticking from the wall. The bars went down into the dark. Ladder. The word was ladder. I put my foot below my foot and my hand below my hand and started going down.

But the words did not like me being there. They got angier and louder. I wanted to block them out by putting my hands over my ears but I could not move my hands. If I moved my hands from the bars I would fall. Sometimes I thought I understood the beginning or the end or the middle of a word but they were only broken parts. As the word parts filled my head I saw bits of things. Not clear pictures but only ugly pieces that went round and round. Smoke and flames and machines and black water from the earth and animal parts and human parts. Things I did not want to see. Things from the older time. Then I saw the dead woods but they were not dead woods then. They were not black and grey but green and green and green.

It was a different kind of green to any green that I had seen. A green from the older time or before the older time. The goodness of it made me hurt. The hurt was worse than any hurt caused by the ugly things.

The green pain filled up my heart as the words filled up my ears. I put my hand above my hand and my foot above my foot and climbed out of the pit and ran back to the light. I ran back to the dead woods hoping that I might see green. But they were only black and grey as they had been before.

The wordmonger was lying with her face against the earth. She looked ugly lying there. I did not want to see her. I took hold of her body and pulled it through the door. Her body weighed almost nothing like an empty bag. I carried on pulling it down the hill inside the earth. I pulled it through the second rusted door and over to the pit. I carried it to the edge and then I pushed it in. It fell into the words and I did not hear it land. The words closed over it and it was gone.

When I got back to our home my other brother was not there. He had returned and packed a bag and not said goodbye. He had not gone to the girl he was in love with lower down the hill but to another town or an area between the towns. Our father sent out men to search but they never found him.

The wordmonger's shop stayed closed. Our father went there every week and came back sad and angry. He no longer swelled and glowed. He even stopped beating us. The big men further up the hill did not invite him to their games. From that point on it seemed he started growing smaller.

When at last our father died all of us stood around his bed. By all of us I mean myself and my sister and my brother but not my other brother. We have not seen him again. Our father breathed up and down and we waited for his words. We waited for his words but he did not share them. His face was like a smooth grey wall and his mouth was like a rusted door. When it closed it stayed closed and perhaps that was better.

My Wife Designs Beasts

❧

My wife designs beasts. This is what she does. And every day I must hunt the beasts through the dark pine forest that surrounds our home and drag their pelts back through the snow to lay before her fire.

She releases the beasts before dawn, when I am still in bed. She opens the door and sets them loose, the beasts she has designed. Sometimes they are reluctant to go, I hear them rasping and moaning out there, and my wife must shoo them away with a broom or pelt them with lumps of coal. And then she brings me hot sugared tea, porridge, thick bread, slabs of cheese, and she makes certain I wolf it all down because she does not want me to stumble, despair or succumb to the freezing wind.

Together we wait for the sky to turn the colour of blood and gold. My wife dresses me for the cold, in my layers of fur and my winter hood and my ropes and my sacks and my snowshoes. She slips leather gauntlets on my hands, and wraps my fingers around the long, slender hunting needle I use to lance the beasts through their hearts and send their bright blood bubbling into the snow.

I set out at a steady pace, following the tracks of the beasts where they leapt, hopped, slithered, crawled, lurched or bounded over the hill, and from there descended into the woods, to merge with the shadows of pines. From their tracks I make assumptions about the forms their bodies have taken. I note the scrape of a trailing wing, the indentation of a horn, the prints of toes or talons or stumps, the drag-mark of a tongue.

Through the threatening firs I plunge with no thoughts in my head. I must chase the beasts to the end of the earth. That is what I must do. My snowshoes crash through deadwood and crunch deeply in the snow. They slither over frozen streams and sometimes I trip and go tumbling down, face-first into whiteness. I pick myself off, dust the snow from my clothes and continue without respite. I do not allow myself to tire. I do not allow myself to pause. There can be no rest until I have the beasts at my needle's point.

It has been this way for a year and a day. Ever since our wedding night, when my wife designed her first set of beasts. Ever since our honeymoon, when she first sent the beasts out into the snow. Ever since she made it clear that she wanted me to deliver their pelts, soft and warm and wet with gore, to where she sits by the fire at night, toasting her feet before the flames.

The tracks run together for the first few miles and then split different ways. They diverge along separate paths, weaving complicated knots through the trees, in an attempt to throw me off and force me to turn back. This means the beasts have heard my pursuit, have pressed their misshapen heads to the ground to feel my thudding footsteps. I imagine they think I can be confused, that I can be made to falter. But the beasts should know I will not be stopped. That the pattern will never be altered.

By noon I have run the first one to ground. Dizzy and careless with exhaustion, it will have paused to catch its breath, sucking the frosted air through its snout, its beak or its swollen purple lips. I fall upon it through a mist of snow. The needle slips through matted fur, rainbow scales or casing of bone. I hear the muffled pop of its heart. Steam pours from the tiny hole. I gently stroke its head as it fades, wiping away its teardrops of blood, smoothing its crumpled feathers.

Deftly, barely pausing for breath, I remove its pelt with the notched, bone-handled hunting knife that hangs at my side. I loosen the muscle and flesh from the bone, and slip its skin from its skeleton as if I'm tugging a woolly jumper off the body of a sleeping child. I roll the pelt up like a rug and stuff it into one of the sacks that dangle from my shoulders. I clean the needle with a fistful of snow, draw breath, and plunge back into the trees. The others will still be far away, pointlessly running.

Deeper into the woods I go, where the trees darken and the ground is littered with rocks and branches. I stagger uphill through the thickets of thorns that tangle my path, tearing into my winter furs, whipping across my face. After hours of pursuit I come upon the second, the third, the fourth, the fifth, the sixth, the seventh, scattered at intervals in the trees, foam-flecked, flanks heaving. Sometimes they have injured themselves, smashed headfirst into the trunk of a tree, or fallen through a patch of ice halfway over a frozen river. Sometimes the joints of their limbs have popped. They might attempt to continue like this, dragging useless extremities behind them, and I will find tattered strips of their skin caught on jagged branches. Sometimes their lungs will have given out. They will be too weak to go on. They are not designed to run too far. My wife sees to this.

I dispatch them efficiently. I don't like to shout or make a fuss. By this point I'm as weary as them, and I take no pleasure in it. Occasionally they try to fight, flailing, bellowing, kicking up snow, but most of the time they await the needle in silence, even expectantly. Sometimes they seem almost relieved. Sometimes I think they understand why their deaths must happen.

It's dark by the time I get back to our home. My body hurts. I see the lights glinting through the trees. I smell the rising wood-smoke. I stamp off snow at the front door and collapse into the room. My wife unwraps my ropes and sacks, tugs the frozen furs from my body. She leads me to the fire, rubs my arms and legs with hot towels, and coddles me in blankets. She bathes my wounds. She brings hot spiced wine. She unfreezes the skin of my face with kisses. And then she unrolls the pelts I have brought, and while I nod off to sleep in my chair she kneels on the wooden floor examining them meticulously in the orange light.

I see the pleasure on her face. I hear her admiring words. I've been doing this for a year and a day, ever since we married. My wife designs beasts. This is what she does. There can be no rest until I have the beasts at my needle's point.

One day I am too sick to go out. I moan as my wife pulls away the covers, and cannot swallow the tea she brings, and gag at the sight of porridge. My skin is glistening with sweat. I lie there and stare at my chest as it heaves, and my heartbeats boom inside my head.

Perhaps it was something I caught in the cold. Perhaps one of the beasts showered me in poison. Or perhaps I didn't eat enough thick bread or drink enough hot sugared tea. When my wife insists I get out of bed, my legs buckle and I fall to the floor. My head feels strange. I don't know up from down. Sweat pools in the backs of my knees.

All morning my wife tries to bring me back to strength, growing ever more impatient as the sun climbs in the sky. She rushes back and forth from the kitchen, trying to spoon things into my mouth. She brews chicken broth, nettle tea, dark medicinal concoctions steeped with forest herbs. She sticks cones of garlic in my ears. She steams my feet in spearmint tea.

She presses hot bowls upon my back. It only makes me sicker.

I swim in and out of nightmares while my wife fusses around me. Beyond the wall I can hear the beasts. They must have gathered around the front door, huffing the air through the crack where the draft blows in. They want to get out but she will not let them go. They begin to shriek, pawing at the floorboards. I can hear their nails raking the wood. The next time my wife leans over the bed, adjusting the blankets I have thrown off, I take her shoulders with my hands and tell her I cannot leave the house. I say she must let the beasts go without me, on this one occasion. She presses her fingers to my lips, instructs me to be still.

I cannot move for days and nights. Sickness spins inside me. My body feels yellow, then black, then green. My fingers have turned into thumbs. My hands feel bloated, full of dense liquid. A heavy stench lies over the bed. My skin is leaking like a cloth. My condensation drips down the walls and windows.

My wife continues designing beasts every night while I am sick. I want to tell her that she must stop, that she must wait until I'm well, or there will be too many.

The beasts are filling up the house. They don't have anywhere to go. They crowd against the windows and doors, desperate for release. The walls shake as they collide with them, the crockery rattles on the shelves. My wife cannot stop. This is what she does. I do not know what will happen.

One night my sickness peaks. I am lost in a storm of beasts. I close my eyes to make it dark. Through the darkness my wife comes. I think it is my wife. A dark shape bending over me, a blackness blacker than the black, devoid of features. She watches me through a mist of dreams. She pinions me with her eyes. I want to touch her, to speak some words, but I cannot move a muscle. She watches me through the long, black night. She never makes a sound. Later I find I can move my hand. My body is starting to function again. I attempt to reach out for my wife but she is no longer there.

I awake to white light streaming through the window. Its brilliance hurts my eyes. I pull myself up to sitting position and wipe frost off the glass. Everything is white outside. The world is clean and cold. Above the boundary of the pines the sky is turning the colour of blood and gold.

My feet find their way to the floor. My fingers grip the bed-frame. My legs tremble, but support my weight. I stagger from the room.

There is silence in the house. The fireplace is cold. A cloud of ash hangs over the hearth and the embers are grey. I cannot remember this happening before. There is no tea, no porridge, no bread. The furniture is disarranged and the floorboards are deeply scored. My wife is nowhere to be seen. A blue and white china plate lies broken on the floor.

The snow is all churned up outside, and a stampede of many tracks, far too many tracks to count, leads towards the forest. They must have had several hours' head start. There is no time to lose. I do not allow myself to tire. I do not allow myself to pause. I am stumbling through the snow, following the tracks of the beasts where they leapt, hopped, slithered, crawled, lurched or bounded over the hill, and from there descended into the woods, to merge with the shadows of pines.

Before I have reached the crest of the hill I am bent double, staggering for breath. I have to drag myself up the slope with my hands turning blue. It is at this point I remember something. My hunting needle is back in the house, in its rack on the wall. I turn my head, looking back down the hill. There is wood smoke rising from the chimney. The door is standing open. Something moves in the white field, and it is now that I see the man, in his furs and his winter hood and his ropes and his sacks and his snow-shoes, hunting needle in gauntleted hands, lift his head from the tracks at his feet and begin to run, in long easy strides, towards me up the hill.

Uncanny Valley

❧

Nights get dark in the valley, but the lights blaze on in this house of ours. We're hooked up to the grid but we still have frequent blackouts. When the power goes down we light paraffin lamps, greasy oil lanterns, thumb-printed candles with moth wings and bits of dead insects sunk into the wax. Solar lamps with a sickly glow. Hungry kerosene torches. We throw all we can at the night. Everything's blazing away.

The house is built of dark pine, with clapboard walls and a roof of tin. A veranda runs along three sides, with four wooden steps going up to the door, and a low oak bench with tree-stump legs, and the tangled remains of a hammock that looks like a long-escaped-from web. That's all there is. A box of light. Beyond this, the valley.

There's nobody else around for miles.

We were building this place for years and years and years.

Lichen grows on the balcony rail, faint vomit-coloured patches like space photographs of dying constellations. One of the side walls is spongy with moss. The corrugated grooves of the roof are clogged with rotten leaves, and pale fern-like tendrils have sprouted, trembling like antennae.

And around us the great silence of the woods, like the silence of a recently departed mansion. I find myself listening to it at night.

If you listen closely, you can almost hear the thud of the last door as it closed. A foot scuffing the welcome mat. The soft click of the latch.

It's just you and me in the valley. It's dark, but we keep the lights on.

The yellow light rushes over the lawn, to the edges of the brush we cut back. It throws spiked shadows across the grass, creates dark sides of pebbles and rocks like dark sides of the moon. Sometimes I carry the bench down there to the jagged frontier of the light. I sit and listen to the silence of the woods with the light tickling the back of my neck. Dipping my feet in the dark.

From here I can smell the cool smells of night, the dampness rising up from the earth. The silent weight of water in the leaves.

The light shines dully on the trunks of trees along the border of the woods. Fish-wet trunks parading into blackness. Sometimes I get out the halogen torch and sweep its beam across the trees, a two million candle-power searchlight punching a hole in the night.

The trunks of the trees scan past like x-rays.

Here and there a single leaf is illuminated, shockingly defined.

Over there a clump of nettles, drooping listlessly. And over there, a nest of brambles with the good blackberries mostly gone.

There's nobody else here. Just you and me. It wasn't always this way.

I know you don't like me to talk about this. About the others that were here.

'I just don't think of it as important,' you say when I try to remind you.

Perhaps it is not. Nevertheless.

If you sit here, at the edge of the light, if you sit quietly, and look slowly, you will see that the blackness is not uniform. It has depth and density, dimensions of varying darkness. There are layers in the night, blacknesses behind blacknesses, pulling your vision ever deeper inwards through the leaves. If you let your eyes be drawn, your pupils seeping with their own dark, if you follow the long curve of the valley rising up beyond the woods, then dimly, you can reconstruct the body of the mountain.

She's up there somewhere, out of sight. Looking down on the valley.

'There's no one there,' you say to me.

Sometimes a thing is so far out of sight you must close your eyes to see it.

She's up there, where the two slopes meet. At the narrow place, the windy place, the place where trees don't grow.

Old Afarensis, bunched up against the cold. Gorse between her toes.

Down the wrong end of the telescope. On the other side of wind and rock and rain and layers of darkness.

Is she lonely, up there in the cold?

She was always lonely.

Can she see the lights of our house?

Our house is a dream she once had.

You stare at the black heap of the mountain, and perhaps you almost remember. You almost remember remembering. But then you hear a sound from indoors – the clunk of a plate on a table, the burble of a radio – and you glance back towards the house. The yellow light behind the window. A kettle has just been boiled. It's cold out here, and the grass is getting wet. The darkness has gone from your eyes. You take one last look at the mountain but forget what it was you were trying to remember, and now you are only looking the way a tourist takes a photograph.

So you get up and go back inside the house. Back to the lighted dream.

'Forget about it,' is what you say. 'That was so long ago. She was here, and then she left, and she can't come back.'

That night we eat dinner and watch a film, and step out for a smoke before bed. Darkness is total in the valley. There's nothing to be seen.

But she was not the only one. There were others too. They came later, and they stayed a long time. Some left quite recently.

'No, they left long, long ago,' you keep saying, with increasing irritation. 'And none can come back, none of them.'

I'm not saying they can come back. I'm just saying they were here.

Africanus, he was here. Don't you remember him? It's difficult, I'll give you that. We can hardly make him out at all, he's only a feeling we once had, an impression of an impression. The taste of dust. Dry hissing grass. It makes the soles of your feet itch. What do you do with a feeling like that?

'Do what you like,' you say.

It's tiring just to think of him. Walking, always walking.

You feel it after you've walked for miles, climbing a long hill whose crest endlessly recedes. About two thirds of the way up the slope, when the muscles in your legs begin to ache, and the ache spreads through the flesh and through the bone.

Or when it's hot and you haven't drunk all day. The memory of water.

He was here, that was him. At some point, he stepped too far. He stepped right off the map and kept on going.

But by that time, others had come. And they kept on coming.

Habilis came, Ergaster came. Clumsily overlapping. Embarrassing uncles with unfathomable habits, leaving their chipped lumps of rock around the garden, in the house, under the floorboards. Discomforting piles of ashes in corners. Edges of flint you could test with your thumb, and never quite draw blood.

Sometimes we still find these items in drawers, underneath the forks and spoons. Stains on the balcony rails. Oddly smoothed pebbles.

They stayed here a long time, so long it seemed they would never be gone. But eventually they left too.

Erectus was here long before. Before we built the house. This was all his once, everything you can see, from one side of the valley to the other, the plunging gulf of air in between. He lived here for longer than any of the others, impossible distances of time, always a pace ahead of the world. But the world caught him up.

He left a deep disturbance in the air. Something that perhaps can never be righted. I have visions of him. Drawing his knees up to his face and moaning, with chattering teeth. Jumping at shadows. A nervous wreck. Startling at sudden sounds. Always peering fretfully into the darkness behind doors. What was it that he thought he saw?

Perhaps it saw him too.

We can still see the path he took, off into the trees. It leads away from our house, meandering into the woods, as if he was blind or confused when he passed that way. It gradually narrows, becomes less distinct. You can follow it for a while until the undergrowth covers it up, the branches close on either side, and suddenly it's not a path anymore, only a half-imagined gap between indistinguishable trees.

It's a path that leads only to forgetting. I wouldn't go down it too far.

'He had to leave. There was no other way,' you say, putting your arm around my waist.

I didn't realise you were in the room. You startled me for a moment.

I grip your elbow with my hand, feeling the skin move over the bone as you pull me tighter. I put my arm around you too. Together we walk out to the veranda and sit on the step, and then you fetch some beer, and we talk a while and then we fall silent and later the sun goes down. It goes down and up and down and up, and the shadows fill the valley and empty and fill the valley and empty again, and we turn the electric lights on and off and on and off in this house of ours. And sometimes, because life is pleasant here, I forget the others.

The others don't forget us, though.

We are a dream they once had.

In the long light of the evenings, we do repairs on the house. It's old, and there's always something to mend. The moss has to be scrubbed off the walls. One of the steps leading up to the door has split, and needs replacing. On the veranda I measure the wood and cut a plank and sand it down, and then hammer it into place. The new step springs a little under my weight. The sawed wood looks too fresh, too bright, so I rub mud into the grain.

One day we paint all the doors in the house. Another we get on the roof with brooms and clear away the rotten leaves. I find a small grey stone up there, idly scratched with concentric grooves, which fits nicely in my palm. I carry it with me for half a day, and then toss it into the bushes.

Later I try to find it again, but sometimes these things can't be found.

Antecessor avoided the path that melts away into the trees. Perhaps she walked a little way down it, stooping and frowning, pushing back branches, and then changed her mind and turned around and came back to the clearing. She spent much of her time scratching holes in the ground, carefully filling them back in again. Making obscure designs in the rubble. Peculiar bumps in the landscape, like tumours. Tramping down her own paths in the grass.

One of these paths leads to our door. The ground is flattened, a trace in the sunlight. You can still see it faintly. The grass doesn't grow so high there, and the small flowers don't grow at all.

'We should put stones down,' you say from time to time, 'so we don't slip in the mud when it rains.'

'We should put a proper fence up here,' is another thing you say.

I suppose we will do these things. We don't plan on leaving soon.

Sometimes I have problems sleeping at night. I wake at two or three in the morning with a sour taste in my mouth, almost a flavour of burning. I get the feeling I've forgotten to do something, and it troubles me. When this happens I leave the bed and wander through the smoke-black rooms. The smell of the house is different at night. The moonlight gleams off sharp things in the kitchen. I sit down at the table and drink coffee.

I try to think about what I've forgotten, but there's no way to catch hold of it. Just a feeling of unease, somewhere between guilt and loss, that contracts and expands when I breathe, pushing up against me.

I get up to rinse out my cup at the sink, and raise my eyes to the window.

There's a black shape standing there. Someone staring in.

Both of us remain absolutely still. I'm not sure if it can see me or not, motionless inside a dark room. We wait to see who moves first.

It has my height, the shape of my body. There's no one there. It has the outline of my shoulder, my arm. The same tensed stoop. The hint of a nose, the gleam of one eye, fearful, half thrilled. There's no one there. It's only my reflection. Of course I really know that. But occasionally, if I stare the right way, if I let my eyes be drawn, I can almost fool myself. I can stand for minutes on end, unable to step away.

If I step away from my reflection, I might disappear.

So it was with Neanderthalensis. The one who stayed until quite recently, despite what you say. The shadow presence in our house, whose life was so nearly our own. Always in a different room, making the floorboards creak. We could hear him breathing through the walls, keeping in time with our own breaths. It was hard to escape the suspicion that every time we walked into a room, a similar someone had just departed, rucking up a rug as he left or repositioning a table, picking objects up and putting them down in a slightly different place, mysteriously and subtly rearranging the planes of our existence.

We called him Lowbrow, Dead-End, Knuckleface, Bones-for-Brains, Tangletongue.

We don't know what he called us. We heard his muttering behind doors, but tried not to listen.

It was a time of being watched, or the feeling of being watched. The tingling sensation of something always hovering in your peripheral vision, looming out of sight as you turned your head. Of footsteps not quite an echo of your own. Items of clothing stretched out of shape. Unfamiliar thumbprints on the mirrors.

Something like the electric whine that tells you a television is on, somewhere not too far away, even though the volume is down and you can't hear a sound.

'That was no way to live,' you say. Your hands are worriedly doing up and undoing a single button on your sleeve.

It had you checking under the bed, throwing doors open, switching lights on.

'Of course it made me nervous,' you say. 'Who wouldn't feel nervous?'

I cannot clearly remember the first time we found ourselves in the same room, but once it happened, it happened again. It couldn't be avoided. Not quite acknowledging each other, shuffling from door to door or loitering at opposite ends of a room that suddenly seemed too small. Neither of us knowing where to look, or what to do with our hands. Like children caught in the indecision between joining one another's game and turning to run away.

We were never quite able to meet each other's eyes. It was embarrassing. To see the resemblance in each other's faces. The sulky mouth and shy, suspicious glances. There was something unpleasant about it, an echo of revulsion.

But we were never quite able to turn our backs, either. We skirted along the walls like crabs, pretending not to notice.

We lived like this for a long time. We developed unspoken routines. I don't want you to forget that.

'It couldn't go on,' I hear you say. Your fingers are picking at your fingernails, scratching the backs of your hands, doing everything they possibly can to avoid being still.

'It was all in the past,' you say, chopping up meat and hurling pieces into the sizzling fat of a pan. Muscles work beneath your skin. Emotional flickers run over your face as if your skin is dancing.

'Why do we have to do this again?' You are furious now, seething through the house. 'He went away. It happened, it happened, don't look at me, don't look at me like that, don't look at me at all.'

Sometimes when you get like this you slam the door of the house and fume your way through the woods, ripping the leaves off trees. Sometimes you lash out at me, slapping and punching. Sometimes you grab me in your arms, crushing our two bodies together with such violence I can hardly breathe.

'I'm alright now,' you say afterwards, glassy-eyed over a bottle of wine. 'Just one of those moods, that's all. Cabin fever. It gets to me sometimes, living out here, the back of beyond, nothing around but woods and trees and endless nights and no lights and no neighbours. It's so quiet, your thoughts go round and round, you can't help getting crazy sometimes. Sometimes I feel isolated. Sometimes I wish we weren't so alone…'

And then you realise what you're saying, and you pour more wine.

I know you're scared that one of these days I will ask you to tell me what happened back there.

Way back, in the rooms of our house. How we came to be alone.

123

But instead I lie awake at night, or sit drinking coffee at the kitchen table, trying to imagine shapes at the window.

I can never ask you that.

However it happened, one day he was gone. I never saw him go.

After him there was only one, and she almost doesn't count. Little Floresiensis, diminutive, resilient as a cockroach. She had been living here all along, out of sight, too small to even notice. When finally she emerged from the hiding place where she'd squirrelled herself away, creeping out to peer and pry, at first we mistook her for a child. We couldn't help laughing. You played a silly joke on her, putting your hand on her head so her flailing arms couldn't reach, and then pushing her backwards onto the floor. She made no sound, but her eyes were tiny glittering balls of hate. After that she kept her distance, working herself into ever narrower places.

Then one morning we woke up, and she was gone as well.

And so we went about our lives, though I expected more to appear.

To this day, none have.

It took a long time to sink in. I won't deny that I felt relief, a sudden opening up of space that was almost giddying. The shadow presences were gone. There were no more shifty avoidances, no more awkward half encounters. We had the whole place to ourselves, the house, the garden, the valley beyond. We could finally be ourselves, we could do whatever we wanted.

I kept walking into rooms and standing there, not knowing what to do.

I still find myself doing this. I can't find the words.

'We are all we need,' you say, locking your fingers in mine.

Perhaps we are. Nevertheless.

Our house feels so empty.

So we tell stories to ourselves. We populate the empty air with ogres, trolls, leprechauns, giants, goblins, yetis, bigfoots, yerens, almas, yowies, orang pendeks, ebu gogos, aliens. To chase away the loneliness, to fill this house in the old uncanny valley.

But we don't believe our own words anymore. The light's too bright. There's no one there.

It's just you and me.

Leaving the Fold

❧

It is dawn in the city of concentric rings. A woman is leaving the Fold and she will not come back. She waits at the gate, which will open soon to reveal the outer zone beyond. On the far side of the wall is greenness, mist and birdsong.

She carries nothing apart from the bag on her back and the suitcase in her hand. The restrictions are strictly enforced; they will confiscate any plastic. Batteries and wearable tech are outlawed too, even rechargeables. There is not much she can take. Not much she will miss.

A crowd of other émigrés waits patiently and quietly, some in small groups but most of them alone. They watch the flaming sky and the sunlight spreading across the wall, illuminating fissures where delving roots have grown. Some stand with their eyes half closed, as if they might still be asleep. She wonders whether she will encounter them again on the far side of the wall. Whether they will be important to her. Whether anyone will be.

'Are you sure?' he asks once again. He stands tragic in his uselessness, hovering uncertainly, and her heart almost breaks for everything that they shared. She doesn't answer, but takes his hand – a farming tool, blunt and strong, the creases of it scored with grime – and looks back across the Fold, at what she is leaving. The green-roofed domiciles with their squared untidy fields, their orchards and their rows of corn, their allotments, poultry, pigs, polytunnels and pastures. It was all she wanted once. It was not enough.

She has lived here for twelve years, eleven of those years with him. In the early days she was very sick, her physiology unprepared for animal germs, or human germs, or dirt in any trace amount. The smells of milk, meat and blood appalled her, as did sweat, most fluids, egg yolk, decomposing food, fungus, physical contact. Adapting to the brutal proximities of that new life, after the sterile habitation she knew as a child, was a systemic shock. Not all émigrés survived; some gave up, some went back. She was stubborn. She endured. With his help, these things became normal.

In the end he took it well: her decision to emigrate once more, to take a further step outwards on civilisation's spectrum. After the furious disbelief, the resentment and the bitterness, came a state of resigned acceptance that both of them recognised as love. He understood that she had to go. He even helped her to pack. Once he suggested accompanying her but they both knew he could not, and it was never suggested again. He is a part of this zone in a way she can never be.

Beyond the Fold, so far away they might be painted on the sky, rise the glass towers of Citadel, spectral and unreal. That is the zone where she was born, before her first emigration. There are no non-humans there, no pets, no pests, no parasites. Meat is grown in vats and the wind is ventilation. Her childhood memories are white: the fluid glide of robotic arms and hovering attentive drones, the trembling of nanomachines, the gleam of surfaces. Her parents were distant mechanisms, functional and benevolent, for whom she felt no more attachment than she did computers. As a teenager, through UV-tinted glass, she gazed at the sprawling hamlets below and dreamed of wood smoke, mud and rain. She studied hard for her escape. But she only got halfway.

'I will wait for you anyway,' he says, almost to himself. 'Even if you will not come back. As I wait for the rains and the newborn calves. We are waiting people.'

'And I will search for you,' she says, 'even if you will not leave. I will search for you beyond the wall. Some part of you might be there.'

He opens his mouth, closes it. There is nothing more to say. They stand together in the orange light, waiting for the wall to open and the émigrés to walk through. She strokes his hand, releases it. It has other duties now. Cutting and felling and trimming and mending and constructing and repairing. It cannot hold her any more. She must walk on alone.

There was once another conurbation here. It exists within living memory, though not for too much longer. The metropolis died from the outside in as precarity prevailed, as the supply chains failed, as the outermost suburbs fell away, as the roads were overgrown. Pastures took the place of lawns, garages became cattle barns. It was the great unravelling and the great returning. But the city's core remained. Immutable in glass and steel, its skyscrapers like granite cones from which everything else erodes, the zone they now call Citadel, calcified at the centre. The Fold surrounds it on all sides, a messy loop of life and death. And beyond the Fold, the Rewilderness. Which is to say, the world.

This is the choice that the city gives, the choice that is her birthright. To decide what life she wants to live, what sort of human she needs to be. Out there she will find no human rules, only the relationships of a natural world she does not know. She will learn. She will start again.

A creak. The gate swings open.

The émigrés gaze through the wall at the pulsing greenness that unfolds, shuffling for a clear view.

It is darker than she expected. The uncut shade of trees.

To the Bone

❧

We didn't stop clubbing the afanc with our paddles until we were sure its back was broken. On this point Reverend Williams had been most specific. 'Don't stop clubbing the afanc, boys, until you are sure its back is broken,' he'd said. 'Merely battering the bugger will not suffice. You must cleave its spine.'

He was sitting on a pony at the top of the first slope, where the track wound up into the mountain. He was wearing a black hat stiff with frost; his spectacles were steamed. His left hand held a small black book, in which his right hand diligently recorded which men were on their way up to the lake, and which men were on their way down.

We quickly climbed the rocky slope that ran up to the first great peak, beyond which the black lake lay. The land below was black and white, with no smudge of colour in between. The rock of the mountain stuck here and there through the drifted snow in a way that resembled porpoises breaking through a wave.

'Don't forget the head!' the reverend called, his voice unsteady in the wind. Already we were high enough above him to make him appear just a black spot in the snow.

There were eleven men from my village altogether. We had played together as children. The anticipation made us children again, tripping each other on the narrow track, flinging echoes off the mountain walls. We teased fat Rhys, who had a face like a trout, that he might be mistaken for the afanc himself and get clubbed in its place. Our spirits were high with the reverend's whisky and the sense of being part of something bigger than ourselves.

But it was a tricky climb to the lake, and soon enough the quietness overtook us. Before we were halfway to the top a light snow began to fall.

We started to ache in our fingers and thumbs. The cold made us shrink inside our bodies, turned us to men once again.

Word of the afanc's capture had spread far and wide. It had reached our village the previous night, and everyone knew that Reverend Williams of Beddgelert was requesting the help of every able-bodied man in the land. Bells had clanged between villages; summonses had gone out. They had even lit the old beacon on the cliff-top at Aberdaron, and now men from as far away as Ynys Enlli had come to lend a hand in the clubbing.

I'd have liked to have been there when the afanc was caught. I think I'd have preferred the beginning to the end. It must have been a powerful sight to see it bellowing on the shore, water spurting from its nose, lashing out with its tail. Chains had been fastened around its body, attached to teams of oxen. It was said that these oxen strained so hard in dragging the afanc from the lake that one of them popped an eye. It was also said that a chain had snapped, the creature had lurched and maliciously rolled over, and a father and son had had the lives crushed out of them.

I'd also have liked to have seen the maiden: the beautiful virgin they'd stationed there to lure the afanc to shore. If I closed my eyes I could picture her, all alone at the water's edge. Her eyes nervously watching the lake, pretty face flushed with cold. Icicles sparkling in her hair, frost on her perfect lips. It was said that the beast couldn't help itself: it had dragged its body from the murky depths, and laid its hideous head in the maiden's lap.

It was also said that the maiden had offered to kiss the man who finished it off, the one who delivered that last blow. This was in all of our minds as we climbed; even fat Rhys, with the face like a trout. We gripped the wooden paddles the reverend had provided, swung them to feel their weight. The paddles felt serious and smooth in our hands. Anything was possible that morning.

Ascending the final uphill stretch, we came upon a party of fifteen men coming in the opposite direction. They had purple faces and small, resentful eyes, squinting like sulky children. They appeared exhausted from their work; their hands were clawed with cold. They demanded cigarettes, which we gave. Few of them looked at us directly.

'Have you come from the lake?' asked Aled excitedly. None of them spoke, but one man nodded.

'And how does it go?' Aled asked again.

'A hard job,' said this man.

'But it's not finished yet?'

'It's not finished yet.'

'And what's the creature doing? Fighting back?'

'Taking it,' the man replied. There was a pause in which no one else spoke. And then they spat their cigarette butts into the snow and resumed their path down the mountain.

We heard the noise before we saw. At first we didn't know what it was. Echoing from somewhere over the rise – beyond which, we knew, the black lake lay in the shadow of the peak – a steady *whap-whap*, *whap-whap*, *whap-whap* that sounded like slush dripping off a roof, or an audience clapping along to music.

'That must be the sound of the beast's great tail, slapping on the water,' I heard Aled say. But it wasn't, as we soon found out. It was the sound of the paddles.

There must have been twenty or thirty men actively clubbing away down there, with many more gathered round, awaiting their turn. The afanc lay in the middle of them all, tethered to the rock by chains. The paddles were going up and down, rebounding off the afanc's flesh, rising and falling mechanically and without passion. The oxen huddled off to one side, dolefully swinging their horns.

The way I heard it related later, the afanc was the length of a barn and as high as an elephant. This wasn't quite true, but it was still big; longer than a cottage or small orchard. At first it looked like an enormous seal, but then we saw the fur around the chops, the sullen, doggy features. It had a fish's tail and fins, while its front appendages appeared to be something between paws and flippers. Its wrinkled muzzle was fastened with rope, and a few blunt teeth protruded. We got up close to look into its eyes; they were open, with an oily sheen. There was no expression in them.

We also passed the two bodies nearby: the father and son who'd been crushed when they first hauled it out. The bodies were laid on wooden boards with their feet pointing towards the lake and their heads towards the mountain. I could see the father's likeness in the smooth face of the boy, and already a little snow had settled on it.

'Where are you boys from?' A short, stubbled man with a brown bowler hat had approached us.

'Near Llanystumdwy,' I told him. He noted this down, and the number in our group, in a small black book like the one the reverend had been keeping.

'You see what to do. It's not dead. We've been keeping this up since yesterday evening. We take it in shifts, two dozen at a time. Some of these boys could do with a rest. Go ahead.'

So we hefted our paddles and set to work. The clubbers wordlessly shifted aside to let us into the circle. I glanced at Aled, Ellis and Rhys and then raised my paddle high in the air, bringing it down hard on the gleaming flank. It bounced straight back, almost leaping out of my hand.

'You got to watch for the bounce,' said the man next to me without breaking his rhythm. 'One fellow smashed his nose.' *Whap-whap, whap-whap, whap-whap, whap-whap.* He let out a hiss with each impact, like steam escaping from a kettle.

I got the hang of his technique, following his swings. It was easy enough to fall into the rhythm, to learn which part of the handle to grip, how high to raise the paddle before bringing it down.

At first I found it enjoyable. It was like slapping a jelly. The afanc's body was thick blubber, like the whale I saw once washed up on Black Rock Sands. The paddles rebounded off the rubbery hide, sending wobbles up my arms and into my shoulders. The regular smacks made the monster's flesh shimmer like the skin of rice pudding.

'Where's the maiden?' I asked the man beside me, glancing at the crowd. They were watching dully, mostly standing, eating scones and drinking beer. Not a beautiful virgin in sight. All I could see was men.

'The maiden went home some time ago,' the man beside me replied. He swung and hissed, swung and hissed. 'She didn't want to see.'

And so we settled into it. First the men on the left side swung, then the men on the right. *Whap-whap, whap-whap, whap-whap, whap-whap.* The rhythm helped us keep it together. I learned to anticipate the bounce, letting the paddle rise and fall like a pendulum, following its own momentum. The snow fell faster, then slackened off. Shadows moved across the lake. The wet slaps echoed off jagged rock walls that had been hacked for slate a hundred years before.

I was disappointed about the maiden, but focused on the job at hand. I was determined to keep pace with the others, to ensure my blows landed clean and hard, that my movements were as regular as a machine. I had never taken part before in a great work such as this. I was proud to be there with the boys from my village, with Aled, Ellis, Owain, Dai – even fat Rhys, with the face like a trout – the best men I had ever known.

We clubbed steadily for an hour and then took a break to rest our arms. My muscles ached initially, but little by little the ache burned away to leave a pleasant warmth, a numbness. The feeling was like after chopping up logs for a fire. We had each brought a bag packed by our mam, with bread, ham and apples. I shared my food with a couple of men who were standing a little way back from the lake, at a spot where we could see right down the mountain to the fields and even – if it had been a clear day – to the sea.

'Reverend Williams thinks the afanc came from there,' I said to the man beside me. 'It got stranded up here when the waters went down. That was thousands of years ago, he says.'

'Well it shouldn't be here now.' The man took another slice of ham, folded it into his mouth.

We returned to work, and clubbed all the way through the morning and early afternoon. The steady *whap-whap, whap-whap* went on. The afanc's thick flesh began to soften and bruise. The paddles gave us splinters. I saw that the ground around our feet was covered in a layer of tiny black spines that must have once bristled from the hide; now all these spines had been snapped off, and the body was as smooth as a slug's.

The next time I took my rest, I walked around to the front of the afanc to examine its quivering face. I could see no change in its expression. Its eyes were spotted with oily blotches; it was hard to tell if it could still see. I held the palm of my hand near one nostril but could feel no breath. Fur hung off its muzzle like wet moss, half torn away. A rope of saliva, or slime of some kind, attached its bottom lip to the ground.

'Keep it up, boys,' called the stubbled man in the bowler hat through a cloud of pipe smoke. 'Eventually we'll soften the muscle, loosen it down to the bone.' He was still standing with his black book, though new arrivals were fewer now. There were still about forty men gathered round; always twenty active paddles.

'We must break that back by nightfall, boys,' he shouted again a little later, when the sun was lower in the sky. The afanc's skin had turned a different colour, become blotched and darkened. My arms were swinging mindlessly, pounding a soft, shining dent in the flank. The motion had become so familiar to me that it felt strange when I stopped.

We kept it up through the long afternoon and into the first shades of evening. The land grew dim; shadows gathered and spread from the folds of the mountain. Snow began to fall again. Despite the warmth of exercise, we had to pull on extra layers, scarves and thick woollen jumpers that had been donated from the villages. The bitter wind whistled through the holes anyway. There weren't enough gloves to go around.

Sometimes the rhythm of the paddles would change. I could almost close my eyes. It went from *whap-whap, whap-whap, whap-whap* into triples like a steam train picking up speed: *whap-whap-whap, whap-whap-whap, whap-whap-whap, whap-whap-whap* and then *whappity-whappity-whappity-whappity* until we lost the rhythm entirely and the sound became a cacophony, like applause. Sometimes it seemed I heard the impact before my paddle actually struck – the way soldiers say it is when you get hit by a bullet – and sometimes it seemed the sound was delayed, an echo in a well. But it didn't matter whose impacts were whose, whose swings connected with which blows. We were working as one paddle now, a machine that didn't know how to stop. I couldn't feel my arms anymore. My hands felt a long way from my body, moving up and down of their own accord. They barely corresponded with any other part of me.

I could feel by the way the paddle connected that the pounded blubber in front of me had changed in consistency; I was making headway now. All the bounce had gone out of the flesh, its tightness had been broken. The paddle no longer jumped back when it hit, but splatted wetly into soft mush, even sinking in a little. The light brown pulp reminded me of rotten pears; of the orchard at home, last summer's pear jam. I had spoiled the skin and was breaking through fat, smashing the muscle to slop. I wanted to work further changes, batter and batter and batter this flesh until it became something else. There was bone down there. I could feel it knocking. My efforts redoubled, the paddle swung faster, pain stabbed into my shoulders and neck but somehow didn't reach my brain; everything seemed far away. The snowflakes spiralled so fast they made me dizzy.

It took me some time to realise that someone was trying to get my attention, and more for my paddle to slow down enough to stop. A voice was addressing me from behind; a hand was on my shoulder. I glanced round from the mess of pulp to see my friends Owain, Ellis, Rhys and Dai, their features as screwed and purple-looking as the men we'd met descending the mountain all those hours before. Rhys had his trout face turned to the ground, and one of his arms was in a sling.

'Dafydd, stop, just stop a second. Dafydd. Dafydd. Hold.'

'Rhys can't use his hand anymore. He can't carry on. We're going back.'

Rhys lifted his right hand apologetically, supporting it with his left. It was swollen from the wrist to the thumb, luridly purple and shining. His arm was trembling.

'I can't move my fingers,' he mumbled at me, staring at his feet. There were tears welling in his small eyes. He moaned a little, and I couldn't help thinking that if the beautiful maiden was here she'd have probably never have laid eyes on a man who looked quite so pathetic.

'We're going back, Dafydd. Are you coming or staying?'

'I'm down to the bone,' I said. 'I can feel it. We can finish it now.'

'We're going back. There's been enough of this.'

'We're there, we're almost at the end.'

'No, Dafydd. There's been enough.'

'All of you are going back?' I asked, feeling the anger in me.

'Aled says he'll stay, if you won't come.'

I looked at my own hands, torn and blistered, rubbed raw in patches. There were splinters worked under the skin that I wouldn't get rid of for weeks. My hands were crabbed in the shape of the handle; it hurt when I straightened my fingers.

'I'll stay,' I said. 'I'm not leaving now.'

'As you like. You keep going.'

They left their paddles in the growing pile beside the two dead bodies. I watched them retreating down the track, growing smaller in the darkness. Fat Rhys shambled in the middle with Owain's hand on his arm. I waited until they were out of sight, motioned Aled to step up beside me, and fell back into rhythm.

There were only half a dozen of us left. Darkness moved up the mountain, seeping into the blackness of the lake. Before the night fully fell and the land around us was swallowed completely, the man in the brown bowler hat organised the lighting of torches, which encircled the afanc to cast shadows across its ruined body. The flames lit the snowflakes from beneath and turned them into nests of sparks. The faces of the remaining men looked like flickering masks. The wide world shrunk to this bubble of light, outside which nothing else mattered.

I concentrated on the bone. After these hours of working soft flesh it felt good to connect with a solid thing, though the impacts jarred my arms. My elbows and wrists absorbed the shocks. The blood in my veins seemed to ache. The sounds of the neighbouring paddles told me that others had also hit bone; they had changed to a hollow *thock-thock, thock-thock*, like axes against a tree. The clubbers were huffing with exertion now, urging each other on. We could feel that we were near the end, and all of us wanted to be the one there first.

'This is the buried treasure, boys! This is what we've been digging for!' The man in the brown bowler hat was holding his paddle like a flag. He had hopped up on the afanc's back, slipping around in the skinless mush, thudding time with the heel of his boot.

'Here's the last nut to crack! Come on, come on!' he shouted later when the beat was a frenzy, *thock-thock, thock-thock, thock-thock, thock-thock*, like one of those drums the Irish use, and the afanc's body was bouncing from the blows. But we had stopped listening to him long ago. Our ears were tuned for one sound, one sound only.

And then it came: the unmistakable *craaack*. We felt it in our bones as well. And at once the paddles stopped.

It was Aled who'd swung the breaking blow. He had been working next to me. His paddle had stuck right there in the spine, wedged between two vertebrae. One by one, we went over to look. The vertebrae were as big as fists. The paddle had been jammed so hard he had trouble pulling it out.

While Aled tugged back and forth, trying to get his paddle back, I walked round to see the afanc's face. It looked bloated in the light of the flames; its eyes were the texture of poached eggs. I bent close to its muzzle and heard a noise like escaping air, a bubbling moan that continued as Aled grunted and shoved at the spine, and then the body shivered and was silent.

'That's it, boys,' concluded the man in the brown bowler hat in the quietness that came next. 'The job is done. Like the reverend said.'

Later, I knew I would be disappointed. I knew I would feel it so keenly that I'd clench my fists and bite my tongue and still it wouldn't help. I had been so close, it had nearly been me; perhaps just a few more blows. But Aled, Aled had got there first. Even without the maiden here, offering herself to him, my stomach would turn with resentment. My oldest friend. Back in the village I'd have to endure him relating this story again and again, while women crowded around, admiring him. It would make me tug the hair from my scalp. The afanc was wasted now.

But I didn't feel that yet. I didn't feel a thing. A wall of exhaustion hemmed me in. We stood quietly. Aled sighed. One man coughed, wiped his hands on his trousers. Another let fall his paddle. The man in the brown bowler hat looked as if he were about to speak again, but then he turned away to fill his pipe.

Some remained standing, some sat down. The only thing to sit on was the afanc. The tenderised flesh sunk downwards with my weight. I wedged my feet at an angle with the ground and leaned back with my arms folded across my chest, allowing my eyes to close. There was pain in my forearms, my wrists, my neck, but it was so distant I felt it might belong to someone else. The fat supported the back of my head like the cushions in a chapel support the knees. It sounded strange to hear no blows, like when a clock has stopped.

It was warm and it was numb at the same time. Snowflakes settled on my face and didn't melt, and I thought of the two bodies lying on planks who cared even less than I did. It was the most comfortable bed I'd ever known. Like a mattress I imagined rich people slept on. One day, I thought, I would sleep on a mattress such as this.

I thought of the beautiful maiden beside me, how her arms would feel. I imagined taking her cold hand in mine, our fingers sticky with the afanc's mush. I wiped a fleck of gore from her hair. My muscles hurt because she'd fallen asleep and was lying on my body. Our skin was stuck together in certain places.

And then, beneath our backs, the mattress moved. All of us felt it: it passed the length of the afanc's body from head to tail. The slow bulging-out of something deep inside, like a trapped air bubble or a thought. As undeniable as that crack. Like something trying to shift itself from one place to another.

None of us spoke. None cursed or even sighed. But one by one we got back to our feet, kicked the snow from our boots, stretched our arms, picked up our paddles where we'd let them drop – and continued clubbing.

Ingredients

❦

Afanc: Welsh water monster; clubbed to death in 19th century
Akkala Sámi: language of the Kola Peninsula, Russia; moribund
Alaotra grebe: bird species endemic to Madagascar; extinct in 2010
Alma: ape-like wild man of Central Asia and Mongolia
Amalekites: Semitic culture; destroyed by the Israelites, Old Testament
American lion: giant lion species; extinct by 11,000 years ago
Ammonite: Canaanite language; extinct by 5th century BC
Anasazi: Native American Puebloan culture; extinct around 1300
Ancient Nubian: east African written language; extinct by 15th century
Apalachee: indigenous language of Florida; extinct by early 18th century
Arctops: gorgonopsid species; extinct around 254 million years ago
Atakapas: Native American culture; extinct by 18th century
Auroch: species of wild cattle; last individual shot in Poland in 1627
Australopithecus afarensis: human species; extinct 2.9 million years ago
Babylonians: Mesopotamian empire; vanished by 6th century BC
Balearic shrew: shrew endemic to the Balearic Islands; extinct in 1945
Barbary lion: North African lion species; extinct in 1960s
Basque-Icelandic pidgin: sailors' language used in Iceland; extinct by 17th
    century
Belgae: Gaulish tribe; destroyed by Romans, late antiquity
Bermuda night heron: heron species; extinct in 17th century
Bigfoot (Sasquatch): legendary humanoid of the Pacific Northwest
Blackbeard (Edward Teach): English pirate; killed in South Carolina, 1718
Bluebuck: southern African antelope species; extinct in 1800
Bo: language of Andaman Islands; last speaker died in 2010
Brigantes: Celtic tribe of Northern England; destroyed in 2nd century
Broad-faced potoroo: Australian marsupial species; extinct in 1875

Broomisaurus: gorgonopsid species; extinct around 254 million years ago

Bunyip: large water monster of Australia

Cabeza de Vaca (Cow's Head): Spanish conquistador; died in 1559

Cahokia: Mississippian culture; extinct since 19th century

Calusa: Floridian culture; extinct in 18th century

Carthaginians: North African civilisation; destroyed in 146 BC

Cave bear: species of large bear; extinct 24,000 years ago

Caucasian wisent: subspecies of European bison; last three individuals shot in 1927

Cephalicustriodus: very large gorgonopsid; extinct around 254 million years ago

Chachapoya: South American civilisation; destroyed in 16th century

Cuban holly: holly species; date of extinction unknown

Cuban erythroxylum: plant endemic to Cuba; extinct in the wild, date unknown

Cuman: Kipchak Turkic language; last known speaker died in 1770

Coptic: ancient Egyptian language; ceased to exist as spoken language in 17th century

Darling Downs hopping mouse: Australian rodent species; extinct in 1920s

Dinogorgon: South African gorgonopsid; extinct around 254 million years ago

Dwarf elephant: Flores island elephant species; extinct 840,000 years ago

Dzunghars: confederation of Oirat tribes; destroyed in 18th century

Ebu Gogos: human-like creatures from the island of Flores, Indonesia

Eel River Athabaskan: First Nations language; extinct in 1960s

Eoarctops: gorgonopsid species; extinct around 254 million years ago

Elephant bird: large flightless bird of Madagascar; extinct around 1200

Esselen: indigenous Californian language; extinct in 19th century

Etruscan: language of ancient Italy; extinct around AD 180

Eyak: Canadian Athabascan language; last known speaker died in 2008

Fir Chera: Celtic culture of Ireland; disappeared in the Dark Ages

Fijian weinmannia: shrub species endemic to Fiji; date of extinction unknown

Franklin tree: tree species of south-eastern United States; extinct in the wild since 19th century

Fung's: supermarket; closed in 1999

Fuzzyflower cyrtandra: plant species endemic to Hawai'i; extinct in the wild, date unknown

Gauls: western European Celtic culture; destroyed in 1st century BC

Giant: enormously proportioned humanoid species

Giant short-faced bear: large North American bear species; extinct 11,000 years ago

Goblin: small humanoid creature

Gorgonops: predatory gorgonopsid; extinct around 254 million years ago

Great auk: large flightless seabird; last individuals strangled by sailors in 1844

Great Zimbabweans: African kingdom; abandoned in 15th century

Ground sloth: huge North American sloth species; extinct by 8500 BC

Guanches: indigenous people of the Canary Islands; destroyed in 15th century

Harappans: Bronze Age culture of north-west India; disappeared around 1900 BC

Hastings County neomacounia: moss species endemic to Ontario; extinct since 1864

Hittites: Bronze Age culture of Anatolia; disappeared in 13th century BC

Huari: indigenous Peruvian culture; disappeared around 10th century

Homo antecessor: human species in Europe; extinct around 0.8 million years ago

Homo erectus: human species in Africa, Asia and Europe; extinct around 70,000 years ago

Homo ergaster: human species in Africa; extinct 1.4 million years ago

Homo floresiensis: miniature human species of Flores; extinct 12,000 years ago

Homo neanderthalensis: human species in Europe; extinct around 40,000 years ago

Ilin Island cloudrunner: cloud rat endemic to Philippines; last seen in 1953

Island Chumash: indigenous Californian language; extinct in 1960s

Inostrancevia: largest known gorgonopsid; extinct around 254 million years ago

Japanese wolf: East Asian wolf species; last individuals recorded in 1905

Javan tiger: tiger species; extinct on the island of Java in 1970s

Kalkatungu: language of Kalkadoon people of Queensland, Australia; extinct in 20th century

Karankawa: indigenous tribe of the Texas coast; last members killed in 1858

Khazars: semi-nomadic Turkic civilisation; collapsed in 10th century

Kipchaks: Eurasian steppe people; destroyed in 13th century

Kushans: civilisation of the Hindu Kush; disappeared in 5th century

Kw'adza: Tanzanian language; last known speaker died before 1999

Laughing owl: owl species of New Zealand; extinct by 1914

Leontocephalus: South African gorgonopsid species; extinct around 254 million years ago

Leprechaun: Irish fairy being

Lusatians: Bronze Age culture in Poland; disappeared by 500 BC

Lycian: language of Anatolia; extinct around 200 BC

Mahicans (Mohicans): tribe of north-eastern United States; driven from homeland in 1830s

Mason River myrtle: myrtle species endemic to Jamaica; extinct in the wild, date unknown

Maui ruta tree: Hawai'in tree species; presumed extinct for over 100 years

Minaean: Old South Arabian language of Yemen; disappeared by AD 100

Moabite: Canaanite language; vanished in 1st millenium BC

Mughals: Indian civilisation; destroyed in 1858

Nagumi: language of Cameroon; one speaker left in 1995

Nazcans: South American culture; disappeared before AD 500

Nendo tube-nosed fruit bat: bat species of Solomon Islands; last known sighting in 1907

Nick Hunt: man; awaiting extinction

Ogre: large humanoid monster

Olmecs: Mesoamerican civilisation; disappeared before 400 BC

Old Church Slavonic: Slavic language; disappeared as a spoken language in 11th century

Old Tatar: Turkic literary language; disappeared in early 20th century

Orang pendek: humanoid creature that inhabits the forests of Sumatra

Oti: indigenous language of Brazil; extinct in 20th century

Pandyans: Tamil dynasty of southern India; ended 1650

Passenger pigeon: American pigeon species; last known individual, 'Martha', died in Cincinnati Zoo in 1914

Phoenician: ancient Mediterranean language; disappeared by 5th century

Picts: Celtic culture of north-east Scotland; disappeared in 10th century

Pig-footed bandicoot: Australian marsupial species; last sighted in 1950s

Prony Bay xanthostemon: Melanesian plant species; extinct, date unknown

Quagga: South African zebra species; died in captivity in 1883

Root-spine palm: flowering plant endemic to Honduras; extinct in the wild, date unknown

Schomburgk's deer: deer species endemic to Thailand; last individual killed in 1938

Scythian: Eurasian language group; disappeared in late antiquity

Sea mink: North American mink species; hunted to extinction in 1894

Seljuks: Sunni Muslim empire; ended in 1194

Skepi Creole Dutch: creole language of Guyana; extinct since 1998

Skottsberg's wikstroemia: flowering plant of Hawai'i; presumed extinct

Small Ted: teddy bear; lost

St. Lucy giant rice rat: Caribbean rodent species; last known individual died in London Zoo in 1852

Steller's sea cow: sirenian species of Alaska; extinct in 1768

Sturdee's pipistrelle: Japanese bat species; presumed extinct since 2000

Sumerians: Fertile Crescent civilisation; collapsed around 1900 BC

Sycosaurus: gorgonopsid species; extinct around 254 million years ago

Syrian wild ass: Middle Eastern horse species; last known individual shot in 1928

Szaferi birch: tree species endemic to Poland; extinct in the wild, date unknown

Taino: Caribbean culture; exterminated in 16th century

Tangut: Tibeto-Burman language; disappeared in 1500s

Tarpan: Eurasian wild horse; last individual died in captivity in 1909

Tasmanian Aborigines: Aboriginal people of Tasmania; last individual, Truganini, died in 1876

Tenochtitlan: capital of Mexica ('Aztec') empire; destroyed in 1521

Thracians: ancient Balkan culture; disappeared by 4th century

Thraco-Cimmerians: culture of Eastern Europe and Black Sea; disappeared in 7th century

Thylacine (Tasmanian tiger): carnivorous marsupial species of Tasmania; last known individual ('Benjamin') died in Hobart Zoo in 1936

Timucua: Native American culture; extinct as a tribe since early 19th century

Toromiro: flowering tree endemic to Easter Island; extinct in the wild since 17th century

Totoro: indigenous language of Colombia; believed extinct, date unknown

Troll: grotesque humanoid being from Scandinavia

Turquoise-throated puffleg: hummingbird species of Ecuador; last known sighting in 1976

Ugaritic: Amorite language of Middle East; extinct in 12th century BC

Ui Liathain: southern Irish culture; disappeared in 13th century

Upland moa: flightless bird of New Zealand; hunted to extinction by 1500

Viatkogorgon: small gorgonopsid species; extinct around 254 million years ago

Wagaya-Warluwaric: Australian Aboriginal language; extinct in 1980s

Wasu: indigenous language of Brazil; extinct, date unknown

Western black rhinoceros: West African rhinoceros species; hunted to extinction in 2011

Wilson River Karnic: Aboriginal language of Queensland; extinct by 2005

Yahuna: indigenous language of Colombia; extinct, date unknown

Yangtze River dolphin: East Asian freshwater dolphin species; believed extinct since 2002

Yeren: elusive wild man of Central China

Yeti: humanoid creature from Himalayas

Yowie: ape-like creature of the Australian Outback

Versions of many of these stories were first published by the Dark Mountain Project. 'The Golden Age' first appeared in *Succour*, and 'Fung's' in *The Junket* online quarterly. 'The Last of Many Breeds' was originally written for the 2016 Remembrance Day for Lost Species, in collaboration with Brighton's ONCA Gallery. 'To the Bone' was performed at Bristol's Tobacco Factory Theatre in 2010, directed by Caroline Hunt. 'Loss Soup' was performed at The Crypt in Bristol as part of Mayfest 2012, directed by Caroline Hunt and performed by Adam Peck, and also adapted for the youth theatre Summer Festival at the Barbican Theatre in Plymouth in 2017, directed by Rosie McKay. It was also used as inspiration for an interactive performance called *The Liturgy of Loss* at the Uncivilisation and Wilderness festivals in 2013, performed by Nick Hunt, Chris Rusbridge, Laurell Turner and Ellie Western.

ALSO BY NICK HUNT

Outlandish
Where the Wild Winds Are
Walking the Woods and the Water
The Parakeeting of London

About Dark Mountain

❧

And so we find ourselves, all of us together, poised trembling on the brink of a change so massive that we have no way of gauging it. None of us knows where to look, but all of us know not to look down...
Our question is: what would happen if we looked down? Would it be as bad as we imagine? What might we see? Could it even be good for us?
We believe it is time to look down.
– *From* Uncivilisation: The Dark Mountain Manifesto

The Dark Mountain Project is a network of writers, artists and thinkers whose work attempts an honest response to the crises of our time: climate breakdown; social and political unravelling; the death of the myths of endless growth and human exceptionalism; ecocide and mass extinction. The project was founded in 2009 with the publication of *Uncivilisation*, a literary manifesto which called for a new kind of 'uncivilised' writing and artwork that tells new stories for an age of endings. The first issue of *Dark Mountain*, a hardback anthology of essays, short fiction, poetry and artwork, was published in 2010 and attracted attention – and controversy – from within the green movement and beyond.

Since 2014, the Dark Mountain Project has published two books a year: a regular spring anthology, and an autumn special issue on themes that have included technology, poetics, the sacred, travel and belonging, fiction and extractivism. From its origins in the United Kingdom the project has grown internationally, with contributors and subscribers from the United States to New Zealand, India to South Africa, Canada to Ghana, Sweden to Australia. From 2010 to 2013 the annual Uncivilisation festival brought together many of the writers, artists and storytellers who featured in the early issues, and inspired further events in the UK and beyond – including smaller festivals, book launches, workshops and performances. The Dark Mountain Online Edition (*dark-mountain.net*) publishes new material every week and is read around the world.

But books remain the project's core, and over the years the issues have featured a diverse array of writers, artists and thinkers whose contributions – including fiction, non-fiction, poetry, visual art and interviews, as well as work that is entirely non-categorisable – have all attempted to navigate the troubled, uncertain times we are in. As the manifesto says: 'The end of the world as we know it is not the end of the world full stop. Together, we will find the hope beyond hope, the paths which lead to the unknown world ahead of us.'

Everything Dark Mountain has published has been made possible through the support and generosity of our readers. Take out a subscription to Dark Mountain and you will get each issue as soon as it comes out, at a lower price than anywhere else. You will also be giving us the security we need to continue producing our books.

To read more about the different levels of subscription, please visit: *dark-mountain.net/subscriptions*

Milton Keynes UK
Ingram Content Group UK Ltd.
UKHW040615060923
428139UK00003B/112